ILLUS. CO

S0-AKS-318

Nordy Bank

SHEENA PORTER

Nordy Bank

Illustrated by

Annette Macarthur-Onslow

London

OXFORD UNIVERSITY PRESS

1964

Oxford University Press, Amen House, London E.C.4

GLASGOW NEW YORK TORONTO MELBOURNE WELLINGTON
BOMBAY CALCUTTA MADRAS KARACHI LAHORE DACCA
CAPE TOWN SALISBURY NAIROBI IBADAN ACCRA
KUALA LUMPUR HONG KONG

First published 1964

The author would like to thank The Society of
Authors and Messrs. Jonathan Cape, Ltd. for
permission to reprint the extract from *The Welsh
Marches* by A. E. Housman, and Miss Rosemary
Sutcliff for permission to reprint the extract from
Warrior Scarlet.

Printed in Great Britain by
W. & J. Mackay & Co. Ltd., Chatham

TO
Freda and John Norton,
Little John
and my God-daughter, Kathleen

CONTENTS

A Camp on a Hill-top

However short a distance he was travelling, Peter always insisted on going up to the top deck. They had nearly missed the bus anyway and Bron, last as usual, was caught off balance on the stairs as it jerked away from the stop. For a moment she felt as though she were hanging in mid air, until she managed to clutch Joe's ascending ankle.

He looked down and smiled at her, saying kindly, 'All right?' She nodded, and followed him quickly to the front seats, where the other four had settled themselves.

They had arranged to meet in Ludlow and afterwards go

out to Bromfield for tea, to make plans for their camp in the
Easter holidays. Anne, the Furnesses' cousin, was staying
with them for the week-end. Her home was in Bristol. Joe
lived on a farm near Church Stretton, behind the long hill
called the Lawley and more than three miles from the main
road. He was really Peter's friend, being in the same form
at school and the same age, fifteen.

The only bus stop in the long village was outside the
Furnesses' house, and as Peter went into the garden a swarm
of spotted dogs descended upon him, pushing and shoving
and staring through the gate inquisitively to see who else
was there.

'Whoever's let you lot out?' he said. 'You worthless
crew! Make sure the gate's shut, Marge. Oh, don't worry,
Anne, they're too daft to hurt anything, and anyway, they'll
all be after Bron.'

Mrs. Furness bred dalmatians. Bron stayed in the garden
with them, being licked by half a dozen tongues at once, and
nudged, and jumped on, while Margery went to ask if they
were meant to be out. They were not and so were put firmly
back into their large pen in the back garden, all of them
remarking dolefully that they hadn't been doing any harm
and why wasn't somebody taking them for a walk?

While Mrs. Furness made the tea, Peter read out a list of
necessary equipment and stores for a camp of about a fort-
night, and Joe made the necessary corrections. Of the six
of them, he was the only one who had had any experience
of camping, but he had done a great deal of it. He had spent
the whole six weeks of last year's summer holiday walking
across Scotland with three more boys, sleeping out every
night.

Anne paid attention to Peter's reading and tried to be
helpful. She was feeling rather out of things, because she

didn't know her cousins very well and had just met Bron and Joe for the first time. She was not at all used to being in the country either, and secretly apprehensive at the thought of the camp. Robin sat still and looked as though he were listening, but he was making up wild adventures instead, in which the camp was attacked at midnight by an enraged bull, or in which he saved Peter from a sticky end in a bottomless bog.

Margery was sitting on the floor by Bron's chair, stroking Lucy, who was enjoying a short nap with her head on Margery's knee. She was the only dalmatian to be a house-dog, because she was Margery's own. Her stud name was Bromfield Beauty Lucilla, but everyone called her Lucy except Dr. Furness, who thought it too short a name for so large and handsome a dog.

Bron was looking round the room thoroughly, as people do when they are genuinely interested in the inhabitants. She saw how the shabbiness of it didn't matter at all, because it was still a pretty room, pleasantly untidy and looking nicely lived-in. The Furnesses had only been in Bromfield for a year; before that they had lived in Canterbury, but already the house looked as though no one had ever lived there before them.

After tea there was a noisy argument about where the camp was going to be held. Everyone crouched round the Ordnance Survey map spread out on the carpet, or crawled about on all fours to see it from a different angle. This distressed Lucy, who didn't like to see humans at eye-level, and she began to bark loudly and push everybody in turn, to make them get up.

Mrs. Furness came in to quieten them, because of the patients waiting for the evening surgery, and immediately began to make as much noise as anyone else. When they

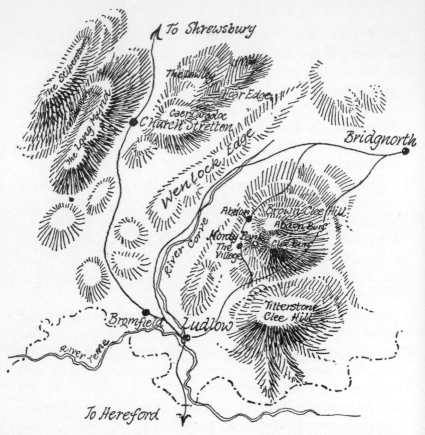

The Stiperstones
To Shrewsbury
The Long Mynd
The Lawley
Caer Caradoc
Church Stretton
Hoar Edge
Bridgnorth
Wenlock Edge
Abdon
Brown Clee Hill
River Corve
Monday Bank
Abdon Burf
Clee Burf
The Village
Titterstone
Clee Hill
Bromfield
Ludlow
River Teme
To Hereford

insisted that the camp must be on a hill-top, she insisted that the Brown Clee was too isolated to be a possible site, even if they could get permission.

'Why not the Stretton hills?' she said. 'They're nearly as high and just as wild, but they're nearer. We could come and see how you were getting on.'

'That's no good, Ma,' explained Peter, 'because Joe knows every inch of them already. No, it's got to be the Clee.'

'Well, if it's *got* to be the Clee, why not the Titterstone Clee? It's such a lovely shape and it's more accessible than the Brown Clee. If you could arrange to be at the Ludlow end, you could be quite near to Bitterley or Bedlam and also be getatable from the main road. The Brown Clee is so tucked away.'

'Yes, but that's what we want, Mummy,' pointed out Margery. 'We don't want to see any more people than we can help. The Titterstone Clee is full of quarries and the Stretton hills are full of energetic summer visitors.'

'And energetic summer visitors' children,' added Peter, 'which is worse!'

'And energetic summer visitors' children's dogs,' added Joe, 'which is worse still, from our sheep's point of view.'

'Well,' said Mrs. Furness, laughing. 'What is the Brown Clee full of, then, that you *must* camp there?'

'Full of quietness and dreams,' said Bron, before she could stop herself, and blushed thickly as all the faces turned towards her, surprised.

Anne giggled and Peter said, 'It won't be possible to guarantee absolute perfect peace, I'm afraid. We'll have to share the hill with several hundred sheep.'

'We've decided then.' Margery stood up to take the eyes from Bron. 'It's the Brown Clee, and Daddy knows a farmer living there, doesn't he? Perhaps he'll help with a site.'

Margery, Bron, and Robin were standing by the garden gate, waiting for the Hereford bus. Bron lived in Ludlow. Joe was already on his way home on the Shrewsbury one, going back beside the River Onny and past Stokesay Castle, towards the hills. The Long Mynd was on the left of the road and the river, but he didn't count it as his, quite so much as the others. The Lawley was most his, because he had been born looking at it, although he was fond of its neighbour, too, the crouching animal shape of Caer Caradoc.

The bus would put him down at the end of his road, where he had left his bike in a farm shed. He sat on the top deck again, in his favourite front seat, and thought about the Easter holiday camp. He was looking forward to it. Nice to be able to show Pete how to do things, for a change. At school he was so much the cleverer that Joe sometimes felt rather left behind. Robin was a nice kid, he thought, and Anne would probably soon grow used to their ways. Margery he liked very much and Bronwen seemed sensible enough, when she wasn't dreaming.

At that moment Bron was getting on to the bus and not dreaming at all. Like Joe, she was lucky to find one of the front seats empty, upstairs. The bus bumped off the verge on to the road again and she waved to Margery, waiting at the house corner.

She had not so far to go. Ludlow was much nearer to Bromfield than was Church Stretton. Bron's father had to move house every two years, because of his job, and she had lived in Ludlow for well over a year now, but she still looked at it with the clear eyes of a new-comer. She could never look at it enough to satisfy herself.

The Titterstone Clee hung poised over the valley, more like a wave than a hill, its crest of black rock reared to fall but never falling. On the right, the town was framed by more hills climbing towards Wales, along Whitcliffe up to Mary Knoll, and beyond, the High Vinnalls. She had seen a stag in the woods there not so long since, while walking with Margery. He had been brown and golden, with antlers royal as any king's crown, and so close that they had been almost afraid. He stood still for what seemed an age, considering them. Then he had stepped aside into the tangle of undergrowth and saplings, and disappeared without the rustle of a leaf or the snap of a twig.

Sitting on the bus, Bron smiled now to think of it and found herself nearly home. The fairy shape of the castle was fading into the darkness and the church tower stood up black over the town. The bus laboured up the hill towards it behind the usual straggle of traffic, and swooped down the other side towards the River Teme. It banged to a halt by the bus stop just in time and Bron fell into an untidy heap at the top of the stairs, along with a comfortably fat lady and a bony-elbowed boy.

2

Do Be Careful!

The wall dividing Bron's narrow bedroom from the living-room was only of thin hardboard. She lay in bed and listened to the level sound of her mother's voice, occasionally rising to a question mark until it was answered by a short sentence from her father. Her mother hadn't wanted her to go to the camp at all, but her father had insisted that she should. Her mother was still arguing about it.

Bron sat up in bed and stared at the sky, which was sunny but still a little grey with sleep. There were neat piles of clothes along the top of the chest of drawers and the empty haversack swung by its straps from the drawer handles. She leaned on her elbow to consider the books in the little bookcase. Margery had told her to bring one, in case it rained a lot, and she couldn't make up her mind which. She had just decided on *Warrior Scarlet*, because it was in a rather battered state and wouldn't show it so much if it did get a little dirtier, when her father put his head round the door.

'Hello!' he said, and came into the room. 'I thought you'd be awake. You've a fine day to start with, at least, and I hope there'll be a regular string of them. You'll have a grand time with Margery and come back looking a real hillswoman, brown as a berry. All right? Anything else you want?'

'Only a chestnut mare, some tropical fish, a dalmatian, a King Charles spaniel, and a large garden.' Bron folded her arms and frowned at him. 'Fetch them at once!'

'No good!' he said, leaning against the door to emphasize his height. 'You're too small to look commanding. You'll have to take up magic and charm them out of me. You look more like Puck than anything else!'

Bron was very small and thin and very dark, and looked smaller than ever sitting up in bed. 'It's nonsense,' she said indignantly. 'What about Nelson and Napoleon? They were tiny!'

Her mother called from the next room that it was half past eight, so her father hurriedly bent to kiss her good-bye and went out.

'Which house is it?' asked Mrs. Owen, who had driven Bron over to Bromfield because there wasn't a convenient bus, and anyway, she wanted to meet Mrs. Furness and the rest of the children.

'Here,' said Bron, and her mother parked the car neatly on the verge.

A head bobbed back from an upstairs window as they walked up the path and the front door opened before they reached it.

'How do you do, Mrs. Owen,' said Margery politely. 'Do come in. Hello, Bron.'

As they went into the hall Mrs. Furness hurried through from the kitchen, untying her apron.

'How very nice to see you,' she said warmly. 'Please excuse me! I'm still clearing up the dinner dishes. That's the worst of having a doctor for a husband, you know. Meal-times are never when they should be.'

'Oh, but I really do envy you, even so. To have a house with your own furniture in it *and* more than three rooms! I do grow so tired of living with other people's colour schemes.'

N.B.–B

Mrs. Furness made a sympathetic noise and led the way into the sitting-room. Lucy, who was lying curled in a large arm-chair, put her ears back and wagged her tail very quickly in a guilty way. Margery went to sit on the arm of the chair and stroke her.

Mrs. Furness noticed the faint surprise in Bron's mother's face. 'Lucy isn't usually allowed on the chairs,' she said, 'but this is a special concession that Margery's persuaded me into, because she's having her first litter in about a week.'

At that moment a car door slammed in the road outside and they heard Joe's voice calling, 'Cheerio then, Fred. Thanks.'

Several feet thumped down the stairs and the front door was opened. Then Joe's voice was in the hall, saying loudly, 'That was Fred. Gave me a lift down.' After a little whispering, the sitting-room door opened quietly and Peter came in, followed by Joe, Anne, and Robin.

After everyone had been introduced, Mrs. Owen began to question Peter on the camping equipment.

'The groundsheets are quite big enough, are they?' she said. 'Oh, and can either of you two big boys swim? You never know what's going to happen, do you? Bronwen catches cold so easily that I have never allowed her to learn.'

Bron blushed, and knelt in front of the arm-chair to stroke Lucy.

Joe looked amused and Peter said, 'Certainly we can swim, and Margery and Robin, too, for that matter. I don't think it'll be necessary though, Mrs. Owen. You could hardly drown in the Clee Brook if you wanted to!'

She nodded and looked round at them all.

'Well, perhaps it will actually do her good to be with so

many of you. She's far too shy.' She turned to Mrs. Furness. 'I really don't know whom she takes after. Neither my husband nor myself were quiet children, and she's so very small and dark, too. My husband's well over six feet tall and as blond as I am. I think she must be a changeling!'

Everyone looked at Bron, who said nothing but began to polish the studs on Lucy's collar.

Margery spoke in her defence. 'Surely she's half Welsh, Mrs. Owen, and that's Welsh colouring, isn't it?'

'Granny and Grandad are Welsh,' said Bron, more red than ever.

A squabble might have developed, but Dr. Furness's dilapidated shooting-brake backed into the drive and the sitting-room rapidly emptied.

Joe and Dr. Furness supervised the packing of the many bundles and haversacks in the space behind the back seat, while the others scurried in and out of the house with them. Finally there was some argument about where everyone was going to sit.

'Well, Joe and Peter, you are lucky boys!' said Dr. Furness, patting them both on the back. 'You'll each have to have a lady on your lap.'

'Not Anne,' said Peter immediately. 'She weighs more than I do.'

Anne giggled self-consciously. 'Then you can sit on *my* lap,' she said.

Finally Joe sat in the front with Bron on his lap, and Peter sat in the back with Margery on his, Robin squashed on one side of him and Anne on the other. Although Robin was only ten years old, he was heavier than Margery.

When they were all safely in, Mrs. Furness wished them good luck and good weather and went back inside the house. Mrs. Owen hovered beside the car, reminding Bron

to get enough to eat, to go to bed in good time, to clean her teeth at least twice a day and to keep her hair dry if it rained. Bron said yes, yes, yes, and Dr. Furness said firmly, 'Well now, Mrs. Owen, we must be away. I hope to see you still here when I return.'

She nodded, stood back from the car, called out, 'Do be careful!' and went into the house.

Joe said, 'All clear this way', because Bron was blocking the driver's view, and they turned right along the main road.

Dr. Furness looked at the crowded conditions in the back through his driving-mirror, and smiled. 'I only hope we don't meet with a policeman in Ludlow,' he said. 'We've an overcrowded car *and* no visibility out of the back window!'

'I don't think we shall, Pa,' said Peter, leaning round Margery. 'We shan't have to go up to the Bull Ring, shall we?'

Margery suddenly leaned backwards and hit Peter hard on the nose, so that his outraged expression encouraged Robin to slight hysterics.

'Oh, I almost forgot!' she said. 'The extra groceries weren't sent out with the order from Newman's. Mother said we were to call for them.'

'Right,' said her father, 'but I'll go round by the back way, and then we should miss the policeman on traffic duty.'

After a short pause, Bron said hesitantly, 'Have you forgotten that it's Thursday?'

Dr. Furness slapped the steering-wheel. 'Drat it! Yes, I had. What do we do now, Margery?'

'Well.' She thought about it for a minute and then said, 'We can manage for a day or so. Perhaps if you have time, you could bring them, or if not, telephone to the shop in the village and leave a message when they do come, and we'll come and fetch them.'

He agreed to this and they passed quickly and safely through Ludlow, or rather, along the edge of it and out on to the Birmingham road. When it looked as if they were going up and over the shoulder of the Titterstone Clee, he turned suddenly left and they drove along in front of it.

None of them, except Dr. Furness, was very familiar with this road. Although it was the Bridgnorth road, the bus went a different, longer way round. So they all stared up at the hill, where the long orange-brown sweep of bracken rose smoothly to the rocky cap between Bitterley and Clee Stanton.

'It's a very flying sort of hill,' said Robin. 'It looks almost as if it could swish along and break on Wenlock Edge.'

No one answered him, which was not unusual, because he did rather tend to get overlooked as the youngest. Bron turned and smiled at him, though, and nodded in agreement.

They soon left the Bridgnorth road, turning off into a narrow, twisting one with high banks and good hedges on top of them. After passing through two small villages and threading what seemed to Anne a regular maze of small roads, Dr. Furness drew up. When they got out, they could see properly where they were.

The Brown Clee rose over them and folded away out of sight on their left hand. A curving flank grew from it immediately above the road and stood up against the sky, looking towards the Stretton hills, the Wrekin and Wenlock Edge.

'That's it.' Dr. Furness swung up his arm in a grand salute to it. 'Your camping ground. Nordy Bank.'

They looked up in silence. He looked at his watch. 'Bless me! If I don't get a move on, I shan't have time for my tea before surgery. I'll just take you down and introduce you to Arthur, then I'll dump you by the roadside and leave you.'

Arthur was a small untidy man with his shirt sleeves rolled high on his thin arms and his trousers too big for him in the seat. He shook hands with them all and said, 'Welcome', as though he meant it. He was a bachelor and now farmed with his brother Edward. Dr. Furness had known him well before his mother died and he had given up the family farm near Bromfield. The campers were to come down to the farm once a day for milk. As it lay just below the road, its roof almost level with it, they had not far to come.

Dr. Furness piled their luggage out on to the verge, jumped back into the car, reversed with short rushes in the narrow road, shouted, 'It's all yours. Get on with it!', waved and drove away at what Mrs. Furness called his 'doctor's pace', fast but not too fast.

They stood and faced the hill and then looked down at
their bundles, which seemed suddenly not to belong to
them. Then Joe stooped, shouldered two haversacks, threw
a tent at Robin and said cheerfully, 'Up we go!'

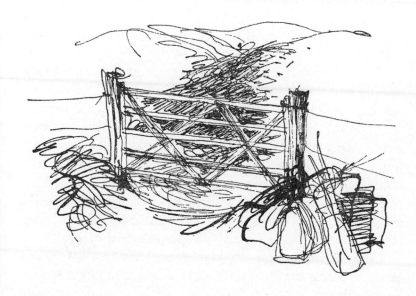

3

The Sleeping War

They all picked up as much as they could carry, but there were still several bundles left.

'We'll just take what we've got up through the gate on to the hill and then come back for that,' said Joe. 'No point in leaving it lying here while we go all the way to the top.'

When they had everything in a heap inside the gateway, beside the green track up through the bracken, he put the tents and haversacks on one side, leaving the kitchen equipment and stores to be taken up in a second load. They had five tents altogether: two large ridge tents and a single-pole tent belonging to the Furnesses, an old ridge tent of Anne's father's, and a single-pole tent of Joe's.

They started up the track to the green head of Nordy Bank, walking between the tangle of rusty brown bracken, beaten down by the winter's snow and wind and rain, partially decayed. The new spring growth lifted small silver-green fronds in the middle of it, still tight-curled into fists, or else with the head tucked down, caught up in the earth and leaving the bare stem sticking up like a croquet hoop.

Joe looked over to the left, to where a tall hedge bordered a stony farm road which wound along the hill-side.

'If we'd any sense, we'd camp there,' he said. 'The top of a hill's the worst spot you can pick, really. No shelter from wind or driving rain, full in the way of hill mist, and no firewood handy. Doubt there's any water, either.'

'Never mind,' said Margery. 'At least we'll have a view.'

They were nearly at the top. The track disappeared before a line of sharp banks and ditches, and they stopped to catch their breath before scrambling up them. Looking backwards, they found they had a view already. Plough and pasture swept down from the Brown Clee to the riverside and on up to hills again.

'Is that the Onny?' asked Anne, pointing to the river.

'No.' Joe put up his hand to keep the sun from his eyes. 'You can't see it very well from here, but it's the Corve. Between this hill and Wenlock Edge, over there, is Corvedale.'

Peter moved on and the rest followed him. The grass-covered banks were slippery, with no bracken to give a hand-hold, but after they found a sheep track it was easier. When Anne asked what the banks were, no one knew but Peter, who said that they were tip heaps from very old quarries that had been grassed over for centuries.

The head of Nordy Bank was flat. Joe gave no one any time to look at the view again, but began to serve out the tent-pegs, which he had carried all together in a canvas bag.

'Shall we put the tents up now, Pete,' he said, 'and go down for the other things afterwards?'

'Yes, all right. Anne, your tent's going rotten, so we'll have that for the stores. You can have Robin's, because he'll be with me in the big one. Where do you think the best place is, Joe? In the middle?'

Joe looked about and then shook his head. 'Better here, I'd say. The fire at the foot of this bank, to be out of the wind, and the tents in a half-circle round it. Then we'll have our backs to the main hill up there, which is where the wind'll be coming from.'

They all turned to stare up at the long ridge behind, crested with the dark woods which warmed the farther side of the hill. Then Joe threw each bundle of tenting on the ground, in its right position, and began to untie his own.

'Oh but, Peter!' said Anne. 'We won't have anything to look at if we're right up against this silly big bank. We shan't see anything but grass!'

'Well, since this silly big bank goes right the way round this particular hump of the hill, I don't quite see what you can do about it. Unless you'd like to pitch your tent right on the top of it, which you'd find rather breezy.' He threw one end of his groundsheet to Robin to pull taut. 'Anyway, you won't be lying in bed looking at the view for long, so I shouldn't let it worry you.'

By the time Anne had fixed up the single pole of her tent Joe had already finished pegging out his guy-lines and unrolled his sleeping-bag. When he had helped her, he went to inspect Bron and Margery's large ridge tent, and found them both busily tugging at the flaps in an effort to tie them shut.

'What's this, then?' he said. 'The ever-open door?'

'It's trying to be,' said Margery. 'I think it must have shrunk since last year. It was all right then.'

'It's the way you've put it up.' Joe began to take it down. 'I can see you're no Girl Guide.'

'I didn't realize that *you* were,' said Margery, looking down at him indignantly. 'I suppose you're going to take it back to the shop to change it, are you? We bought it in Canterbury, so you'd better hurry or you won't be back by dark!'

Joe didn't answer, but took out the poles and laid the tent flat over the groundsheet. Then he tied the door flaps neatly together and began to put the tent up again. Bron went to help him, had a short fight with Margery when she tried to stop her, and finally they both helped him.

'There you are,' he said. 'Lesson number one. Fee one guinea. Always tie the flaps first or they won't hang right.'

Peter was putting up the store tent. A shower of small stones flew out from Anne's that she had picked up from underneath her groundsheet. Robin was carefully making a fireplace below the bank. He had cut out a square of turf with his knife and was making an edging of small stones. Margery and Bron went up to admire it, because they knew how much he wanted someone to notice.

When they had fetched up the second load from the gate by the roadside and put everything neatly away, they went down for the third time. Joe and Peter went back to the farm to ask Arthur about water and to collect some milk. The others gathered firewood along the tall hedge at the bottom of the hill. They found plenty, because the hedge was old and ragged, and were making a wood-pile at the side of the store tent when Peter and Joe came back.

Peter carried a bucket of water in one hand and the full milk can in the other. Joe carried a large sack over his shoulder.

'This is going to be a semi-civilized camp,' announced Peter. 'Arthur thinks it would be quicker in the long run if we use a tap and the etcetera down at the farm instead of being primitive up here. We can fetch water for the cooking when we fetch the day's milk. It does seem stupid to keep carting enough water up here to wash six people, and we can have the use of the tap in the old dairy that they don't milk in now.'

'That's the white shed on the left of the gate,' added Joe. 'He gave us a sackful of rough stuff from his wood-pile, too, to help out. He's a nice chap, isn't he, Pete?'

They had tea, explored briefly around the flat area on the top of Nordy Bank, and then sat in a row on the bank in front of the camp, to watch the sun going down behind the hills.

The rays fell level across the sky, became tangled behind

the higher hill-tops and broke up into an orange dazzle of light. The near slopes of the hills were deep in shadow and mist began to grow out of the ground and lift among the trees. For a time Corvedale glowed like a deep stage, set with a series of backcloths folding into the distance and each lit by a spotlight. Then the sun fell lower down the sky; its rays tipped and tilted; began to fade from orange to pink and caught in its searchlight beam high clouds which until then had been invisible.

To the north-west were the long humps of the Stretton hills, backed by the Stiperstones and Corndon, wild and lonely hills on the very border of Wales. Westward their view went down by the Corve and the Onny, over Stokesay to the quiet falling woods of the Clun Forest, and beyond to the Welsh mountains and the growing dark.

They sat for some time in silence, each looking at different things although their view was the same. Robin deliberately blurred his eyes until the hills began to move against the sky, pretending they were alive and frightening himself. Anne was frightened anyway, of the darkness behind them on the Brown Clee. Peter was trying to work out what you would see now if you were sitting on Corndon Hill and looking towards the south. Joe saw the lighted windows of the farms and guessed at the identity of the people behind them.

Margery saw the whole sweep of encircling hills and thought of their centuries, ages of time and ages of men, when the hills had not changed at all.

'I wish I knew that poem,' she said quietly to Bron, 'because it just catches that sort of strange watching and waiting feeling of all this.' She waved towards the west. 'It begins,

"High the vanes of Shrewsbury gleam
Islanded in Severn stream . . ."

but I can't remember any more. It's called *The Welsh Marches*.'

> ' "The sound of fight is silent long
>   That began the ancient wrong;" '

Bron said quietly, hesitated, and then continued:

> ' "In my heart it has not died,
>   The war that sleeps on Severn side;
>   They cease not fighting, east and west,
>   On the marches of my breast.
>
>   Here the truceless armies yet
>   Trample, bathed in blood and sweat;
>   They kill and kill and never die;
>   And I think that each is I." '

Her voice had risen fiercely and they all leaned forward to look at her.

'Savage!' said Peter. 'You sound quite like a native!'

Bron began to blush, as she always did when she realized that people were watching her.

'It's not me,' she said quickly. 'It's the words. Housman wrote it.'

They looked forward at the hills again. Anne looked backwards at the dark.

'I suppose it was a bloody stretch of country once,' said Peter thoughtfully. 'What with the Celts against the Romans, and both of them against the Saxons, and then the Civil War. Still, I don't have any sinister watching and waiting feeling, as you put it, Marge.'

'Oh, I do now,' said Margery, staring at the fading sunset. 'I *feel* the sleeping war.'

'And so do I,' said Bron.

4
Nordy Bank

The first cold daylight filtered into the tents, being transformed into sunlight in the two double ones because their canvas was yellow. Before she was used to camping, Margery had often dressed in a rush and hurried outside expecting a heatwave, only to find the sky full of clouds and no sign of the sun at all.

Anne's tent was white and when she woke up she shivered, because it looked so cold. She stared round the tent for a second and then closed her eyes. As soon as she had done so, she realized what she had seen, crawling over the groundsheet almost at the level of her face, coming towards her.

For an instant she lay rigid and then, struggling out of the sleeping-bag, she leaped across the groundsheet, tore the flaps open, and ran screaming over the wet grass.

Joe shot out of his tent in his pyjamas, just as Peter appeared from his. Anne disappeared into Margery's.

'What on earth's bitten that girl? I thought someone was being murdered, but there's no blood!' Peter went over to the girls' tent and poked his head inside. He then went into Anne's, came back to Joe, and put a worm into his hand. 'I suppose you can't blame her too much. She was only half awake when she saw it.'

Joe looked down with amazement at the pink worm twisting on the palm of his hand, which had sent Anne screaming with fright into Margery's tent at six o'clock in the morning.

'Frightened of a *worm*, though, Pete! There's enough meat on her to make half a million worms, but she's frightened of this little beggar!'

Bron appeared as he spoke. 'Where is it?' she said, and seeing it, picked it up gently from his hand. 'She's just not used to worms,' she added in a matter-of-fact voice, seeing that they were both amused. She carried it away into the bracken.

'That's more like it!' said Joe, with satisfaction. 'She may be shy, but at least she's got some sense. Well, I suppose that now we're up, we may as well stay up.'

Anne redeemed her character at breakfast time by proving a good cook, and afterwards astonished Joe by cutting up the fresh meat they'd brought with them from Bromfield for a stew. He couldn't see the difference between one small worm in its skin, and gory beef that wasn't. In fact, the worm seemed preferable for fastidious souls, as far as handling was concerned.

'We'll have to find a shop somewhere,' she announced. 'Aunty said that the groceries from Newman's that didn't come included the butter, the sugar, and the tea. We can't do without those and we really need them before dinner.'

'There's a shop in the village,' said Peter.

'Good. I've always wanted to go there,' said Joe, 'because someone told me that there's a sizeable stream running right down the middle of the street.'

Everybody wanted to go then. Anne said that someone would have to stay to watch the stew. It had to cook fast for a while and then be moved mostly out of the fire to just simmer. Joe said that he would, but the others thought it fairer to draw lots for it.

N.B.–C

Peter held five long pieces of straw in his fist, and one short one. They each drew one out and Bron had lost.

'I'll stay with you then,' said Margery. 'You won't want to be on your own.'

'No, it's all right.' Bron looked round at the hill. 'I really don't mind at all. I'll read *Warrior Scarlet*.'

'If you feel like being useful, you could dig shallow drains on each side of the tents,' said Peter. 'That'll lead any rain-water we may have behind the camp, instead of making a quagmire of the fireplace. Although I suppose the water running from the bank will do that in any case.'

Anne gave a last anxious look at her stew, which had not yet come to the boil, and followed the others to the road gate. Bron went down with them to send them on their way.

She sat on the gate to watch them out of sight and stayed there for a while after they had gone. It was still early in the morning. The only sounds were of a tractor buzzing some-where on Arthur's farm and a sparrow chirping monoton-ously on the farmhouse roof. Bron thought that if she had been a better shot she could have thrown stones down the chimney from where she was sitting. That made her think of their own fire and of Anne's stew, perhaps boiling al-ready, and she turned back up towards the camp.

Before starting to read *Warrior Scarlet*, which she knew she would find it difficult to stop doing, she took Joe's trowel and obediently began to dig shallow drains on both sides of each tent, as Peter had suggested. It was a windy day and rather cold, although the sun was trying to find its way through the hurrying clouds.

When the skin of her neck and arms began to prickle, Bron thought that she must be colder outside than she felt inside, and went to fetch a cardigan. The sun came out then and she sat down on the bank above the camp to feel it

warm on her back and to watch cloud shadows moving
across the valley below her.

Usually she never minded being alone, and in fact liked it
more than being with other people. Now she felt strangely
uneasy and couldn't stop herself turning every few moments
to make sure that no one was standing behind her. Of
course, no one ever was. Sitting on the bank-top, she could
see anybody approaching long before they reached her.
Bron told herself this, and then said it aloud for comfort.

The words blew away. The wind whispered along the
hill-side and rattled through the dead brown bracken. The
grass on the flat head of Nordy Bank stirred as though it
were alive, seeming to billow like a green carpet with the
wind beneath it.

She said it to herself again. 'I'm quite alone. No one can
be watching me, because there is no one else here.'

She thought of what Margery had said yesterday, that the
hills seemed to be watching and waiting and somehow,
remembering. She looked up at the Brown Clee, darkening
with cloud shadow as she stared at it. It was such a big hill;
it wasn't watching *her*, little Bronwen Owen sitting in its

lap to look at the view. The Brown Clee was watching
Wales and all the hills between.

Sun chased the cloud shadow away across the face of it,
and Bron felt suddenly warm again and ready to read
Warrior Scarlet. On her way to fetch it, she looked at the
stew and moved it further to the edge of the fire. She stared
down at the fireplace for several minutes, hesitated, and
then walked slowly away to pick up the trowel.

When they had passed through it in the car, the village
had seemed quite near to Nordy Bank. But now the
twisting road appeared to turn away from it as often as it
turned towards it. They had viewed the Brown Clee from
several angles before the road seemed to be able to make up
its mind where it was going and to take a determined line
straight towards the village.

'Well!' said Joe, as the first group of houses came into
sight. 'I think there must surely be a nearer way than this
one.'

'I'll ask at the shop,' replied Peter, who, as usual, appeared
to have taken charge of the expedition.

They found the stream running down the middle of the
road easily enough. The shop was more difficult to find.
The stream took the whole width of the road for some
distance, running fast and cheerfully and managing to look
not at all out of place, before sliding off across the verge
and deepening between grassy banks.

They walked the whole length of the village, but found
only houses and a church and nothing that looked in the
least shop-like. Finally Peter went up to a woman hanging
washing out in her garden and she explained to him why
they had not noticed it.

'It's round at the back of a bungalow,' he said, rejoining

the others in the road and turning down the way they had come. 'It's the one nearest to the church and she says there's a sign to show you which way round to go.'

They found the church easily and then the bungalow. The only sign visible was a small neat arrow painted on to a board on the wall.

Following this, they walked carefully and in single file along a narrow gravelled path which wound between the flower beds. Many summer visitors, hunting ice cream and crisps, lost their nerve at walking all round the bungalow in front of private windows, only on the strength of an arrow, and turned tail. Bolder ones, however, stood still to stare in at the windows, observing the life of the natives.

When Robin had just remarked quietly that this bungalow seemed to be six-sided, the path came to a halt before french windows and inside was not a sitting-room, but a shop. Peter was the last one in and shut the door behind them. A bell rattled loudly and continued to rattle, bringing a very small woman scurrying in.

'Push her hard, will you, my dear,' she said, pointing to the door. 'Give her a good old shove and she'll quieten hersen.'

The rattling stopped abruptly and they all turned from looking up at the bell to look down at the shopkeeper. She was very plump as well as very small and wore a fluffy yellow angora beret to hide her curlers. Since she had on a jumper to match and very dark bright eyes, she immediately reminded Margery of a chicken and she wished that Bron were there to see her, too.

While she put together their groceries, she chattered busily about the village, the hill, the bad winters they had, and the variety of customers in the summer.

'We do get they walking ones; can't hardly be seeing some

of them, they do have such great packs up on th'shoulders. Then there's all the folk from Birmingham, piling out of they big buses and gawping all round. Mostly they don't come in here, though, us having no shop board up, but all of our regular folk don't need any board to find us by. We've been here past thirty year.'

She paused for breath and congratulations. Peter seized the opportunity to say that it must be getting near dinner-time, and could she recommend any nearer way to Nordy Bank than the way they had come, round by the road. After asking where they had all come from and introducing herself as Mrs. Pritchard, she took them through her garden to a stile at the bottom of it.

'You're quite welcome to come this way through,' she said, and pointed out their direction. 'I dare say you'll be there before your friend well expects you. It's not far by this way over.'

So they came up to the camp from the side opposite to Arthur's farm and they did surprise Bron. She was squatting beside the fire and didn't see them walking across the head of the hill.

'She looks smaller than ever now,' remarked Peter. 'You could almost take her for one of the little people!'

'Don't be ridiculous!' Margery punched him in the back, cross because Anne was giggling in a silly way. 'It's the way she's sitting, that's all.'

'Yes, that's right,' said Joe, 'and she's clever to do it. I fall over after a couple of minutes.'

When they all looked at him inquiringly, he added, 'Squatting on the flat of both feet, because usually you squat on your toes.'

Bron was astonished to find herself surrounded by people not apparently interested in the stew, but all attempting to crouch down as she had been doing. Robin had the most success, because he was the thinnest and lightest, but the others found that to do it for long exercised too many unknown and unused leg muscles. Margery laughed a great deal at Anne's efforts, in revenge for her laughing at Bron.

Then Joe saw the fireplace.

'Well, look at this!' he exclaimed. 'Somebody's been busy! Just what we need, especially when rain-water drains down from that bank. It's bound to rain some time and then that ground'll be good and soggy.'

Bron had built a neat raised fireplace, with a hearth of smooth pebbles and shallow walls. The stew-pot was balanced on the corner of two walls and a long narrow stone which had been laid across as a support. They all admired it.

'But where did you find these stones?' asked Peter. 'They're all pretty nearly the same weight and shape. Has Arthur got a dump of them?'

Bron stared at him and then at the fireplace. 'No,' she said, hesitantly. 'Not from Arthur.'

'Where, then?'

She stood up and looked round, but didn't answer, so that Peter turned to Anne and tapped his forehead in a rude way. Margery saw him do it and frowned at him. Bron walked out of the camp and went along beside the bank to a place some distance away, where it curved sharply towards the middle of the hill.

'Here they are,' she said, pointing to a hole in the side of it where a large square of turf had been neatly cut out. That part of the bank appeared to be made of the smallish stones, piled loosely together.

'A pebble mine!' said Margery. 'How useful!'

Peter was determined to be awkward. 'But why on earth

trail all the way up here to dig them out, and have that distance to cart them back again? Why not dig for them beside the camp?'

'I don't know why,' said Bron. 'I just *felt* like digging here.'

5

A Grey Alsatian

The afternoon was still as sunny as the morning had been. It was still as windy, too, with a wildly erratic and blustery wind that swung and shouted in the lilac bushes at the bottom of the Furness's garden. At one moment the lilacs stood still and expectant, and the next were bent double before it. Mrs. Furness was weeding beneath them and felt their roots straining in the ground.

What a wind! She thought of the tents high up on the side of the Brown Clee and hoped that the children had had the good sense to make them doubly secure. Peter was surely old enough to be trusted now, though, and Joe seemed a very down-to-earth character. Margery and Bron made a pair of dreamers, but she knew that they were both reasonably sensible. Anne was *too* sensible, she thought, and smiled to herself as she remembered her quite obvious admiration for Peter. Robin would be all right with them; he wasn't too excitable.

She piled the last of the torn weeds into the wheelbarrow and moved away towards the rubbish heap that would finally be a bonfire. Nice not to have to bother about getting ready the usual big tea for five. She might even have time to take some of the dogs for an extra walk. That reminded her of Lucy, and the fact that she would probably be hungry again by now. She went indoors.

Lucy had given birth to her puppies in the night and, because it was her first litter, was extremely proud and

anxious. She didn't like even Mrs. Furness, of whom she
was very fond, to look at them too often. When the door
opened she looked up and thumped her tail in the large
shallow wooden box that was her bed, then stepped slowly
out to stretch and yawn and see what was put into her dish.

When Mrs. Furness knelt beside the box, Lucy swivelled
round until she could watch what was done with the
puppies and eat at the same time. There were five of them.
They were all white, because their dalmatian spots would
not begin to appear until they were more than two weeks
old. Four puppies had a glow of pink skin shining through
the white silkiness, but the fifth and smallest looked like a
very old young thing. It seemed to have shrunk inside its
skin, which was not a healthy pink but a dull yellow, and it
lay listless and apart from the others, which were tumbling
and scrambling in slow motion, searching for their mother.

Mrs. Furness picked it up. 'Sad little thing,' she said.
'I'm afraid that you'll not be enjoying life for long. You
look very poorly.'

Lucy hurriedly finished eating and went to nudge her hand, wanting the smallest one to be back with the others. Mrs. Furness put it down.

'I suppose that I ought to get rid of you before Margery sees you and is upset about it, but it seems wrong to take away your small chance before you're old enough to fight for it. Well, Lucy, I'll leave you in peace. I must ring up and leave a message for Peter; they'll probably go down to the village for groceries in the morning.'

When she telephoned to the shop which was also the post office, Mrs. Pritchard explained that the children had already been in, but said could she take a message?

'Oh, what a shame!' said Mrs. Furness. 'I quite thought that they'd leave their shopping until Saturday. I should be very grateful if you could tell them to ring Bromfield as soon as they can, to have some good news. It is most kind of you.'

Mrs. Pritchard said that not at all, it was a pleasure, and she'd send the message up to the children via Arthur at the farm, via the postman.

At the same time on that same afternoon the Bristol train moved noisily from Shrewsbury station. Its next stop would be Hereford, before it ran into Wales and out again, towards the Severn tunnel and the estuary.

The sun shining full in at the carriage windows was hot, without the wind that went with it. The luggage van was hot, too, and airless, particularly full because of the extra travellers and extra mail-bags that went with Easter time. The guard was cross. Hadn't he got enough on his hands without that great alsatian sitting there staring at him? Savage brute snarled every time he walked past it. If it hadn't been muzzled, he reckoned his legs would have been in ribbons by now.

The alsatian was a young dog, with fine intelligent eyes, and a thick coat of wolf-grey fur brindled with black on the flanks. He snarled because he felt the guard's fear, because he was himself confused by the strangeness of his surroundings, and because his was a trained ferocity. He was an army dog.

His handler travelled with him, the only man for whom he felt affection and whom he obeyed instantly. At that moment Corporal Smythe was down at the front of the train, queueing for tea in the refreshment car. It had been a long journey. The alsatian was soon to lose even this one friend, because he was being escorted down to the dogs' reform school run by the National Canine Defence League.

The Royal Army Veterinary Corps had trained him for almost two years. Now he had to be *un*-trained, to be taught normal behaviour, good manners and reliable gentleness. Partial deafness had developed that made him unsuitable for work with the R.A.V.C., and he had been given an honourable discharge. If the canine reform school could not succeed, then he would be destroyed.

The train rattled on: down between the Stretton hills and past the big yards of the sheep market at Craven Arms, down by Stokesay Castle and the race-course at Bromfield, towards Ludlow. The alsatian, tethered by a thick leather leash between mail-bags and piled boxes of yellow chickens, laid back his ears and snarled silently. He was irritated by the loud and continuous cheeping of the chicks, as well as bewildered by the noise and movement of the train.

There was a sudden hiss of brakes and each carriage lurched backwards in turn, jostled by the buffer of the one before. The train shuddered to an unscheduled halt in Ludlow station. Mail-bags tumbled down on to their sides, and an enormous trunk slid heavily from one end of the van to the other. The guard opened the door.

'What the heck's the matter?' he said, seeing the station-master running along the platform towards him. Two porters followed, pulling a large cart loaded with wooden boxes.

'Shan't keep you long,' panted the station-master. 'It's an SOS job. Bristol hospital wants this machine urgently. Been made here at Stackham's and rushed through the tests overnight. Are you full?'

'Yes, I am!' snapped the guard. 'Hardly room to breathe in here as it is. Well, come on then. Let's get it all shifted round.'

The first thing to be shifted was the alsatian. The guard reluctantly unstrapped the leash from the iron bars at the end of the van, and tried to pull the dog to one side out of the way. At that moment a porter stumbled against the piled boxes of chicks, which slithered and banged down on to the floor.

The alsatian pulled forwards; the guard stepped backwards; the leash flew up out of his hand and the dog was gone. Some seconds had passed before the four men managed to make their way to the door, climbing over luggage and trying to avoid stepping on the chickens which had escaped from one of the boxes.

There was no one on the platform, because no train was due. There was no sign of the dog. The train stood at the station for a quarter of an hour, while the machinery was loaded into the van, and while Corporal Smythe searched the two fields behind the station buildings, whistling and calling again and again.

'Not what you'd call obedient, is he?' remarked the guard irritably when the handler rejoined the men standing impatiently on the platform.

'If he heard, he'd come.' Corporal Smythe stared angrily at the guard. 'If you'd thought to fetch me before meddling with him, it wouldn't have happened. You knew where I was. He's used to no one handling him but me.' He turned to the station-master. 'What are those yards on the other side of the line, please?'

'Well, that's the live-stock market and it covers a good area too. But he'll surely not have crossed the line without anyone seeing him?'

'I doubt it, but he can move like a bullet when he wants to, and as quiet as a cat. I'll have to leave the train and contact the police now, I think.'

The guard nodded emphatically. 'It might be an idea. I dare say two or three of the passengers would like to get to Bristol before nightfall!'

The train moved away and Corporal Smythe was escorted to the police station by a railway clerk on his way home. The search went on all through that side of the town until late in the evening and even then the soldier carried on alone, losing his way in the unfamiliar streets and whistling until his lips were dry.

When the alsatian leaped down on to the platform he had turned left, away from the hissing engine and down on to the track. Passengers on the opposite platform, waiting for the Shrewsbury diesel, were all up by the ticket office and not looking that way in any case. The signalman could easily have seen him, but he was working out safety margins between the delayed Bristol train and others following on the down line, and he didn't.

The dog ran on beside the track, not moving at full speed in a leaping gallop, but low to the ground at a kind of fast loping trot. He passed above the Birmingham road on the

bridge and then, just before the main line crossed the River
Corve, turned right along the railway track which led up to
the quarries of the Titterstone Clee. This was no longer in
use.

Away from the noise of the train and the noise of the
town, he ran more slowly, and when the track turned across
open fields he left it and went steadily on into the country-
side.

The sunset was as wild as the day had been. Wisps of
red-brown cloud swirled across the sun and the bronze sky,
and the wind began to be cold and unfriendly. At least,
Bron thought that it felt so, and she had been silent all
evening, because she felt unfriendly herself, although for
no reason. The camp was closed early for the night, as they
had been up almost at sunrise because of Anne's worm, and
in any case were all tired after so much walking.

At Bromfield the puppies were sleeping through their
first night of independent life, and the smallest one appeared

to be a little stronger. Lucilla seemed to give it special attention, as though she had understood the words that Mrs. Furness had spoken aloud while holding it pityingly in her hand.

The alsatian was well beyond the small village of Middleton, drinking from the Ledwyche Brook, which ran down from the Brown Clee to join the Teme. He was drinking clumsily, because of the muzzle, and already beginning to feel very hungry. He was lonely, too.

6

The Fortress on Nordy Bank

Peter was the last one to go down to the farm to wash and went round the yard to the house afterwards to collect the milk. Arthur and his brother were sitting in the kitchen with the door open, eating their breakfast. Although it was only eight o'clock, they had already been working for more than two hours.

' 'Morning,' said Arthur.

Edward nodded, without bothering to look up. Peter stood in the doorway and swung the milk-can. 'It was a wild night, wasn't it?' he said.

'Surely. And another wild day coming.' Arthur turned in his chair to point to a small churn standing in the corner of the kitchen. 'Help yourself. There's the dipper.'

While Peter did so, Arthur stared thoughtfully at his back.

'You made any plans for this morning then, have you?' he asked.

'No.' Peter replaced the lids on the churn and the milk-can and walked across to the door. 'Nothing special. Why?'

'Just thought you might like to earn a bit of extra. We've to whiten the cow-stalls before that Government chap gets along here. He's up round Bridgnorth just now and he'll not be long. Waste of our time, Ted and me doing that; there's plenty else needs doing. You six'd soon knock it off. Give you five bob apiece.'

Edward looked up then and nodded in approval. Peter considered.

'Yes, all right. I rather like slapping whitewash about and I don't suppose the others'll mind.'

They didn't, and went down to the farm straight after breakfast. It was a satisfying job, to see the rather dingy cow-shed growing cleaner and lighter.

'Why is it so grey, though?' Anne was disappointed, expecting the walls to glow with whiteness immediately. 'It isn't thick enough. Let's mix it stronger.'

'Dopey!' Peter rather unkindly whitewashed her nose and chin. 'It's wet, that's all. It dries white.'

Anne retaliated with unexpected spirit and slapped her brush on to his hair. This made Peter cross, because he always found it rather more difficult to take jokes than to make them. He went outside to their sink to wash it under the tap.

While he was gone, Joe began to question Bron again about the reason for her digging in that particular part of the bank for stones for the fireplace.

'But I've told you!' Bron stared at the wall in front of her. 'I just went, and they were there. I didn't think about it at all.'

'It's odd. That bank really looks to be made up entirely of those even-shaped stones and so presumably all the banks are. So Peter's ancient quarry theory must be wrong. If they were quarry tips, the banks would just be rubble.'

'Of course he's wrong!' Bron's voice was confident and surprisingly contemptuous. 'We made the banks; they were built up; they were not just thrown there to be out of the way of a quarry.'

Joe stared at her in surprise. The others continued whitewashing in silence. Only Margery was really listening to what was said, and she couldn't hear very well because she was working on the opposite wall.

'What do you mean by "we"?' asked Joe. '*We* made the banks.'

Bron said nothing in reply, but only looked at him briefly before walking across to begin on the last wall, at the end of the shed. Joe stood still in astonishment. What a look! When Peter had told him that Bron was coming to the camp he had described her as 'shy, and as quiet as a mouse'. Well, Joe thought to himself, whitewashing thoroughly into the corner, I just don't agree with him!

They had finished well before twelve o'clock, and so Anne had plenty of time in which to cook dinner before anyone became unmanageably hungry. Joe had brought a huge square pan for frying, which fitted nicely on to the low walls that Bron had built round the stone hearth. They had bacon and eggs, fried tomatoes, fried bread, and fried potatoes.

'Very nice,' remarked Peter, when they had cleared the things away and were ready to set off. 'Just the sort of lovely unhealthy meal we're never allowed to eat at home.'

'Yes, that's the worst of having a doctor for a father,' explained Margery. 'We always have to eat dreadful healthy things, like wholemeal bread and prunes.'

'Not all the time?' Anne was horrified.

'Yes, absolutely all the time,' said Robin solemnly. 'We never eat anything else but wholemeal bread and prunes.'

'Except when we have visitors, of course. Then we eat ordinary food to be polite.' Peter looked so serious that Anne quite believed what he said.

Joe was smiling and Margery turned to Bron to share the joke with her, but she didn't seem to have been listening.

They had decided to walk straight up from Nordy Bank to Clee Burf. The Brown Clee hill was long, waisted in the

middle and with two heads to it. Clee Burf was the one nearer to Ludlow. Abdon Burf faced towards Bridgnorth and was the larger of the two, almost one thousand eight hundred feet high.

The wind came bowling over the top of the hill and swooped down on them, so that walking against it was quite an effort. Anne gave up following in Peter's footsteps and went to the back of the line, where she imagined that she was a little sheltered by the other five. No one bothered to talk. The words had to be forced out against the wind and were reduced to a whisper in any case.

When they reached the top they stood in a row and got their breath back, looking down the other side of the hill. Normally there was a good long view to the east, but today it was shortened by mist and low cloud.

'We'll be having that soon,' Joe shouted, waving towards it.

Peter nodded and grabbed Robin just in time, as a particularly strong gust almost tumbled him over. They turned to look towards the Titterstone Clee, the head of which was almost directly to the south.

Margery suddenly began to laugh at Peter, who caught one of her flying plaits and tugged it. 'What's up with you, then?' he shouted.

She pointed to his hair, which was standing stiffly up all along the parting as the wind blew on to the side of his head. 'You're a new species,' she shrieked. 'A crested boy!'

Anne and Bron turned their backs on the wind. They both had short, straight hair and it was whipping to and fro across their faces, stinging their cheeks. They all ran down some distance below the ridge, to sit and look at the view westwards, while the wind swept on over their heads. Sheltered from it, the sunshine felt beautifully warm.

To the west they looked over the rounded hills of the Clun Forest into Wales. The horizon there and to the north was reasonably clear, and Robin began a heated argument with Anne, who was convinced that she could see Snowdon.

'You might as well say that you can see Ben Nevis, while you're about it,' he said in disgust. 'Your geography's worse than Marge's, and that's saying something, isn't it, Pete?'

Peter didn't reply. He was staring down the way they had come, at Nordy Bank.

Seen from above, the pattern of the banks stood out clearly, encircling a large area, guarding it. They were quite obviously not refuse tips from old quarry workings; they were fortifications.

'Well, look at that!' exclaimed Peter, pointing downwards. 'We've put our tents in the right place, haven't we? Bang in the middle of a Roman fort!'

There was general excitement, in which only Bron did not join. Margery began to wonder if she was homesick or not well or something, because she'd hardly spoken all afternoon.

'It's not Roman, though, Pete.' Joe cast about in his memory for a vague knowledge of prehistoric civilizations which was in there somewhere. 'Not Roman,' he repeated. 'It's Stone Age.'

Peter turned to argue with him, but Bron said loudly and unexpectedly, 'No. You are both quite wrong. It is Iron Age.'

'And why's that?' Peter didn't mind being contradicted by Joe, but Bron was a different matter. She had always seemed very shy when he had seen her at Bromfield; now she was becoming altogether too cocksure and conceited, he thought. 'How do you know so much about it?'

'I do know.' Bron looked at him as she had looked at

Joe in the morning. He was as surprised as Joe had been.

Since she didn't appear to intend explaining further, he said again, 'Why is it Iron Age?'

'The Romans built their forts in advance of a line, each one farther out into the wild, like beads on a string. They were not haphazard builders, and roads joined all their buildings. Each fortress was connected with a base, and was set in a valley or on high open ground to be accessible to it. That,' she looked down to Nordy Bank, 'was placed so as to be as difficult of access as possible.'

They were all impressed by this and even more by the way in which she had put it. However, Peter still felt like arguing.

'Hear ye, hear ye, Bronwen Owen, the Talking Textbook!' he said, ringing an imaginary bell. 'Well then, having proved it's not Roman, now prove it's not Stone Age either.'

'The valleys were not safe in the days of the old people, because the forests harboured the wolves, and so they built their camps on the hill-tops, too. But they were used to pen the sheep and cattle in safety behind stockades, and not to keep men out. The banks were not so high nor the ditches so deep, and the entrance was just a gap and not defended—so.' Bron pointed to the side of Nordy Bank nearest to Arthur's farm.

Now that they looked closely at it they could see the short curved banks thrown up before the gateway, the two sides of which were turned inwards to force the attackers into a dangerous confinement. When you were walking on the hill itself, the shape of this gateway was not so obvious, because the ditches were choked with bracken and the banks worn down by wind and rain.

Margery looked sideways at Peter and could see that he

was getting cross, so tried to think of something to say which would be interesting enough to change the subject. As she turned towards Abdon Burf she saw grey fingers of mist grope over the ridge and then begin to tumble and slide down towards the valley.

'Look, Joe,' she said. 'It's arrived.'

They all went back to look over the top of the hill, and as they moved up from the one side, the mist moved up from the other. It passed between them and drifted on, leaving them shivering in a cold, grey and viewless world.

'Like Marley's ghost!' said Margery, and was pleased and relieved to see Bron nod and smile in her usual way. She walked across to her.

'How did you know all that about the forts?' she asked. 'Have you been reading books about it?'

Bron shrugged. 'I don't know. I can't remember, but I suppose I must have.'

They went quickly down towards Nordy Bank, taking a circular world of changing grass and bracken with them. The camp looked comfortless when they got there, but improved very much when Joe managed to reawaken the fire and piled it high with some of Arthur's logs.

After tea they went for a long walk along the road, in the opposite direction from the village gathering firewood as they went. When they were making plans for the next day Joe asked if they would mind helping him to make a supposedly Iron Age type of house.

'Only a small one,' he said. 'I'm just curious to see how they might have managed to keep the roof on and how warm they were. We could just do a miniature one, really. We don't want to be carting rocks about for ever.'

They agreed, and each carried a stone back up to the camp, as a token of their good intentions.

'You won't have much bother with know-how anyway, Joe,' said Peter. 'Here we have our Resident Consultant Iron Age Architect, Miss Bronwen Owen.'

Margery looked quickly at Bron, to see if she was offended, but again she didn't seem to have been listening.

7

Spears, Sling Stones, and Wolves

The next day was Sunday. The wind returned in the night, but as it blew the mist away back over the hill, nobody minded. It strummed in the guy-ropes and billowed through the tents, chasing the clouds across the sky at a great pace, so that cloud shadows swooped up Corvedale.

Bron and Margery were sitting on the top of the bank to watch them while Anne stirred the breakfast porridge anxiously, afraid that it might be lumpy. If it was, Peter refused to eat it. Peter and Joe were drawing house plans and trying to decide on building materials. Robin was finishing the drains that Bron had started beside the tents.

It was beautifully clear and sunny, and all the hills stood out sharply against the sky. Margery was doing enough talking for two and so did not appear to notice Bron's silence. Bron was feeling confused and rather peculiar. She knew that she had been awkward and argumentative yesterday, and felt the same today. She didn't *want* to be and usually never was, but somehow the words seemed to be in her mouth and to come out before she had thought about them. They weren't *her* sort of words at all.

After breakfast they all scattered down the hill-side, looking for stones, except for Joe, who went over to the farm to ask Arthur if they could chop some branches from the hedge by the roadside. This did not serve as a stock barrier, as it had been left standing several feet inside the new post and rail fence bordering the road. They also wanted permission to cut some turfs to lay over the branches to make the roof of the hut.

When Joe came back from the farm carrying a chopper they went down to hear what Arthur had said.

'We can have some.' Joe stood back to look at the hedge with a professional air. 'I'm to cut them out though, as I've done a fair bit of hedge laying. We mustn't take too many, because the sheep gather here off the hill when the snow's lying, to be fed, and it makes a windbreak for them. No turfs, though. We'll have to make do with bracken.'

By mid-morning they had three piles—of bracken, hawthorn boughs, and stones—in the camp. The pile of stones was much the smallest.

'That won't take us far,' said Peter, and then added, 'Why didn't we think of it before, though? While we've been grubbing about for rocks, there's that pebble mine of Bronwen's lying idle. We can sink a shaft!'

Bron turned round abruptly. 'No! Leave them alone! They may be needed.'

'Needed?' Anne looked down at the even-shaped stones that made up the hearth. 'What ever for? We don't need another fireplace!'

'They are gathered there for the slings. They must be left alone.'

They all stared at her in amazement.

'What do you mean, Bron?' asked Margery quickly, seeing that Peter was going to be sarcastic again. 'What slings?'

Bron looked rather bewildered for a moment. 'For use against the raiders,' she said slowly, after a short silence. 'They are always heaped on either side of the gateway, to be ready. They are the sling stones.'

No one spoke. A curlew cried in the quietness and a gust of wind flustered in the bracken. They suddenly heard the bells that had been ringing for ten minutes past in the churches of the valley, the sound brought up on the wind to the Brown Clee and carried away again.

Joe turned to Peter. 'Well, they'd not really be a lot of use,' he said. 'Too small. I've got a better idea. You all go on collecting for a bit and I'll try to work something out.'

He stood up on the bank and stared down the hill. After a few minutes Peter joined him there. Then they began to move the building materials down into the ditch between the steep top bank and the smaller second one.

'What are you two doing?' asked Margery, as she and Bron came into the camp with their arms full of old bracken.

'We've changed our minds,' said Joe, 'and we're going to build it in the ditch. Then the banks will make the two side walls and we shan't need half so many stones.'

Margery began to say, 'A good idea', but Bron stopped her by saying loudly and rudely, 'Don't be so ridiculous!'

Joe looked astonished and Peter angry. 'And what's your objection this time?' he said.

'If the house is to be outside the fortress, why bother with any defences? Only people of the Stone Age lived in the ditches beyond the banks! What would protect you from spears and sling stones?'

Peter and Joe looked at each other in amazement. Margery, trying to avert a quarrel, smiled and said, 'Well, that's true! But still, what we want protection from now for *our* hut, is the wind. You know how it tears across the top of Nordy Bank, with nothing to break the force of it.'

Bron looked round at the banks, broken down in some places and half covered by the bracken.

'You should have seen it as it was.' She spoke quietly, in a strangely sad way. 'These banks were steep and high then, and topped by the palisades. The ditch between the banks was deep, as well, and muddy with stagnant water. It's only a ghost of what it was.'

Peter suddenly burst out laughing. 'You slay me! From the way you talk about it, you'd think it was just a few years ago, instead of about two and a half *thousand*!'

Bron didn't reply.

'Well!' said Joe, cheerfully. 'If the Stone Agers built their huts in the ditches, then that's what we'll do. It'll just be a Stone Age hut instead of an Iron Age hut, that's all!'

Peter and Joe continued with the building of it in the afternoon and Robin helped, but the girls rather lost interest. Anne began to write a letter to her parents in Bristol and Bron and Margery read.

As they were having their tea, Arthur's big sheep-dog bustled into the camp and Arthur followed it. The dog went straight across to Bron and stood beside her, his tail flagging gently to and fro.

'You're honoured, you are.' Arthur sat down stiffly on the bank. 'He doesn't take much notice of people, in general.'

'Bron has a sort of magnetic attraction for dogs,' explained Margery. 'Would you like a cup of tea?'

'Thank you, but I mustn't take too long over it. I've come to bring a message, just. Mrs. Pritchard says you've to ring your Ma up from the shop first thing, to have some good news. She told Thomas the postman; he told Edward; Edward forgot all about it until now.'

'That'll be the puppies, I expect,' said Margery excitedly. 'Thank you.'

While Arthur drank his tea, Peter told him about the way in which they had realized what the banks around the camp were and Joe told him how he intended to make the hut reasonably waterproof.

'If this wind keeps up and grows at all in the night, somebody might be left with no tent over their head,' he said, 'and then we'd be glad of it.'

Arthur admired what had been done already. They had planted three strong forked branches along the middle of the ditch, and laid a straight branch across them. Smaller boughs sloped from this on to the bank-sides, and one end had been filled in by a thick and rather untidily built stone wall. The doorway had yet to be made at the other end and bracken woven between the hawthorn boughs.

After Arthur had gone, Anne helped Peter and Joe with this. Robin was trying to make a kite from sticks and brown paper and Margery helped him. Bron continued to read *Warrior Scarlet*.

When it was too dark to see properly, the hut builders came to join the others by the fireside and Peter and Joe each began to make a kite, too, because it was such good weather for flying them. As it grew darker the firelight grew brighter, and so Bron was able to go on reading.

Peter suddenly thought that she looked lonely. He had been rather sarcy to her this afternoon, he supposed, and perhaps she hadn't deserved it. After all, she did seem to know what she was talking about.

'This is nice and peaceful,' he said cheerfully, 'and that looks like a good book, Bron. Will you read some out loud to us while we're kite-making? If it's about the Bronze Age, it is more or less appropriate to Nordy Bank.'

Bron was pleased. She had thought that Peter was annoyed with her. 'Shall I begin at the beginning?' she asked. 'Yes, it is good. It's my favourite one of Rosemary Sutcliff's.'

'Not the beginning.' Peter made up the fire with the last of Arthur's logs. 'Give us a quick outline of the plot and then go on from where you've got to. Might be time to finish it then.'

She read for half an hour and they all enjoyed it. When she had reached the part where Drem, the boy, is attacked by wolves while guarding a sick ewe, Anne shivered and moved round to the other side of the fire, beside Bron. She didn't like sitting with her back to the bank: her shoulders tensed with the expectation that some creature was waiting to leap down on to her, out of the darkness. Now, at least, she could see it coming!

Bron continued reading: ' "The moon swam out suddenly, free of the scudding, curdled cloud into a lake of clear sky—and in the sliding silver light, something moved on the smooth whiteness of the snow before the quarry mouth. Something dark, and running low, like a great hound. But it was no hound; and behind it came two more. Now that the moment had come it was almost a relief; and as the wolves swerved in their tracks and headed in towards him, Drem began to yell; yell and throw the lumps of chalk that he had gathered. That might frighten them back for a while, but not for long. If only he had some means of making a fire—fire to singe their hides! The great grey leader flinched from the lump of chalk that caught him on the shoulder, and gave back a little. But they were famine-driven . . ." '

There was a swift and almost silent movement on the bank, beyond the circle of firelight. Anne stared upwards, her mouth screwed into a grimace of fear, before she threw herself back and clutched at Bron. Then she screamed.

Bron saw it for one unending second before it disappeared: a grey wolf poised above them, eyes gleaming

red in the firelight. She dragged herself away from Anne, seized a branch from the edge of the fire, and leaped to the bank-top.

The night was not fully dark. The wind-washed starry sky gave a vague shape to the contours of the hill, showed the outline of the second bank below the rampart and the patches of bracken dark against the grass. Nothing moved on the slope.

Bron held the torch high above her head and made a long cry, a long alarm, of the one word, 'Wolf!'

The confusion behind her was so great that no one seemed to hear what she shouted. Anne was shrieking with fright and sobbing in the intervals. Peter was helpless with laughter. Robin was giggling, but ran up on to the bank nevertheless, not wanting to miss anything. Margery was trying to

quieten Anne and not to start laughing herself. Only Joe
had jumped down into the ditch and was running to and
fro in the bracken. He had seen nothing at all, because he
had been sitting with his back to the bank, but he had had
that strange feeling between his shoulder blades that made
him sense something alive behind him.

It was a long time before the camp was quiet. When everyone but Bron had laughed at Anne for long enough, she
was persuaded that what she had seen was the moon shining
through a cloud. Bron said nothing, but straightened the
page that had crumpled when she threw the book down,
and continued reading the thirteenth chapter of *Warrior
Scarlet*. Then they went to bed.

Half-way down the long slope of the hill below Nordy
Bank the alsatian lay in the bracken. He had been without
food for three days. His cheeks were sore where he had
scratched and scraped and rubbed at the leather muzzle.
The thick leash trailed beside him on the ground.

His physical condition had not altered too much as yet:
his sides were more hollow and his shoulders more promi-
nent than before, that was all. But he stared round nervously
and sniffed often into the wind, because his growing deafness made him distrustful of the strange silence. His eyes
showed plainly his fear and loneliness.

8

Auction Monday

In the morning they all went down to the village. Because they went the shorter way, through the fields, and because Margery hurried them along, they arrived at the shop before it was open.

They sat in a row on the fence at the bottom of Mrs. Pritchard's garden and heard the church clock strike a quarter to nine. As they sat there they saw two empty livestock trucks go up towards the hill and two full ones come down carrying sheep. From a field farther along the road came a confusion of baas and barks and strange human cries.

'What on earth's that man saying?' said Margery. 'Is it a Brown Clee dialect, or is he talking Sheepish, or Muttonese, or whatever sheep talk in among themselves?'

Joe laughed. 'It's plain Shropshire, and the dogs understand it even if you don't. He's late getting away.'

'Where's he going to?' asked Anne. 'Has he sold his sheep to another farmer, or a butcher or somebody?'

'Not yet. It's Auction Monday—and he's going to Ludlow.' Joe looked rather as if he wished he were going, too. 'Dad's taking two score to market this week, and I expect Mum'll go in with him for shopping.'

Mrs. Pritchard knocked on the window to them then, and opened the shop early and unofficially. Margery phoned through to Bromfield at once, while the others talked to Mrs. Pritchard.

'I'll buy a huge box of chocolates to celebrate,' announced Margery on her return. 'Five puppies, and Mum thinks that four will be good ones. I shall be so rich!'

Because Margery owned Lucy, looked after her, and bought her food out of baby-sitting proceeds, the puppies belonged to her, too.

'If we can get into Ludlow somehow, Dad will bring us back in the car. He can't fetch us, because he's too busy, but Mum wants us to collect those camp groceries and I want to see the puppies. She says she doesn't mind if we get a lift in, but she made me promise that we'd all stick together.'

'We can surely hitch a ride in a market truck,' said Peter.

Joe shook his head. 'Not if we stick together. They might get three in at a pinch, but that's all.'

'We'll have to wait for a car, then,' said Margery.

'Well,' suggested Mrs. Pritchard, 'there *is* the bus!'

'A bus?' They were all astonished to think of a bus coming up to the village.

'Of course we've a bus,' said Mrs. Pritchard indignantly. 'Twice a week we've a bus, Mondays and Wednesdays. It'll be stopping by the church there, just about nine fifteen. It travels round a bit, mind, but it'll be down by Ludlow at something after ten o'clock.'

Bron had hardly spoken all morning and now surprised everyone by saying, 'If you don't mind, I'll stay at the camp. I've got rather a headache and I think the bus would make it worse.'

They all tried to dissuade her, and when they couldn't, began to argue about who should stay with her, for company. Finally, Robin said that he would.

'Oh no, you mustn't,' said Bron quickly. 'I know that you want to see the puppies. I shan't at all mind being on

my own, and I can have dinner ready for you when you
come back. Or will you stay there for dinner?'

Peter said that they wouldn't. 'Pa will be coming this
way on a call after morning surgery, I expect, and that's
why he said he could bring us back.'

They walked down to the church and joined a chattering
crowd of about ten women who were gathered there. In
the ten minutes that they waited for the bus, however, three
passing cars drew up and carried away seven of them, to
save them the fare, and then a lorry loaded with sheep took
the eighth.

'That old bus'd better be on time,' remarked a middle-
aged lady carrying three baskets, 'or us'll all be gone.'

It came into sight as she spoke; Bron left the others and
walked alone up the road to Nordy Bank.

They certainly saw a great deal of Shropshire which was
new to them. The bus zigzagged to and fro, going uphill
to small villages and down narrow valley roads to even
smaller ones. It grew rapidly more crowded and more
noisy. Everyone knew everyone else and there was a steady
basic buzz of conversation, with occasional shouted in-
quiries flung from one end of the bus to the other rising
over all.

Robin was soon held entranced by the reminiscences of a
very old man who came and sat beside him. As he climbed
slowly on to the bus, a general cry had greeted him, 'How
are you then, Harry?' And Harry had replied merrily, with
a wide smile that stretched out his silver moustache,
'Blossoming, I be.'

Robin had begun to make polite conversation and been
astonished to learn that Harry was ninety-five years old,
had spent many years in Africa and India with the army,

had emigrated to Australia and returned when he was sixty to take over his father's farm. Now he was going into Ludlow to see how well the sheep were doing that his own son had taken early into the market.

When they reached the town they had over half an hour to wait before the Shrewsbury bus would take them on to Bromfield, so went down Corve Street with Joe to try to find his father at the auction. They soon did so.

Mr. Catlin was a short man and broad-shouldered, with the dark hair and the high cheek-bones of many of the Welsh border people. Joe was very like him, although already a little taller.

'Well, I'm surprised to see you here.' Mr. Catlin walked back towards the road with them to lose the market noises. 'Run you off the hill already, have they?'

Joe laughed. 'Not yet, Dad. We're waiting for the Shrewsbury bus, on our way to Bromfield. Mum with you?'

'No. She thought Church Stretton could fix her up for groceries today, seeing that the big eater is out of the house.'

They stayed at the auction for half an hour, and then said good-bye to Mr. Catlin and caught the bus at the bottom of Corve Street.

When they arrived at Bromfield, Margery had run into the house before the others had even reached the garden gate. Lucy shook off the feeding puppies when she saw who came into the room, and welcomed Margery as joyfully as if she had been away for a year, instead of only three days.

The others came to admire the puppies, but when Peter saw a small crowd of children passing in the road he went straight out again. There was one man in the middle of the crowd, his shoulders a little stooped, as though from repeated inclination of his head to hear what children were

saying. Everyone carried a haversack or bag of some sort,
that looked as though it might be heavy.

Anne went to the window to see what Peter was doing.

He was standing talking to the man, while the children wandered on down the road.

'Whoever's that?' she asked. 'The Pied Piper of Ludlow?'

Joe and Robin put down the puppies they had been holding and went to see.

'That's Mr. Norton,' said Robin. 'Our fossil man.'

'What he means,' said Joe, 'is that it's the curator of Ludlow Museum, who knows almost everything about fossils and is quite famous. He gives talks to children from all over the country.'

Anne looked as though she would consider this somewhat boring. 'Then I suppose that's a fossil-hunt,' she said. 'They mostly seem to have a hammer as well. How dull, carting a lot of rocks about.'

'It is not!' said Robin indignantly. 'We get such good fossils that they almost look as though they're going to start moving again. You can just imagine the creepy things crawling along through the slime.'

'And the ferns waving in the forest,' added Margery, 'and there are some huge corals, too, and lovely patterns made by bark.'

Peter turned to come back into the house then, leaving the Pied Piper to catch up his children.

'Well, Bron was right,' he said, sitting down on the floor beside Lucy's box. 'I expect she's been talking to Mr. Norton about it. She's often up in the museum all day in the holidays, isn't she, Marge? Along with half a hundred others.'

'Right about what?' asked Margery. 'Nordy Bank being Iron Age?'

'Yes. He says there are a lot of camps round here, made when the earlier Celts moved back before the Belgae towards the mountains. Those pebbles probably are sling stones, as well. They've uncovered big dumps of them inside the ramparts of some of the camps.'

'Waiting for the attack that never came,' said Margery.

Then Lucy bit Anne's thumb because she tried to pick the smallest puppy up from between her front paws, as she was washing it, and brought everyone's attention back to the present day.

Bron had not enjoyed being alone. She didn't really understand now why she had not wanted to go into Ludlow. She had been looking forward to seeing the dalmatian pups, because she had heard that they were born spot-less. But, down in the village, she had suddenly felt that she did not want to leave the hill. The headache had been only an excuse.

Now it was half past twelve and the dinner was almost ready. She had washed two lettuces, hard boiled six eggs, and opened a tin of corned beef. This was being difficult about sliding on to the plate and clinging stubbornly to the sides of the tin. Bron slid a knife round the sides and it clung stubbornly to the bottom instead. She began to shake it hard, but stopped suddenly, with the certainty that she was being watched. She looked up, and put the tin down.

The grey alsatian was crouched on the rampart, drooling with hunger, his ears laid back and his tail curved between his legs. They stared at each other without moving. Then the dog dropped his eyes to the tin of meat lying beside the fire and a desperate, pleading whimper came from him.

Bron called softly, 'Come, boy. Come to me. Oh, poor dog, poor dog!'

The alsatian crouched lower to the ground, his belly brushing the grass, and began to move warily, grey and wolf-like, down towards her.

Bron stood still to give him confidence, and then stooped slowly to pick up the tin of meat and cut some out from it. Her hand closed on a log. She leaped backwards, behind the fire. She screamed, and threw the log, and then another and another. She continued screaming the one word which would come into her mind, 'Wolf! Wolf!'

The alsatian had gone, sliding over the rampart swift and soundlessly. Bron stood quite still for some time, an expression of shame and bewilderment on her face. When she went to look down the hill-side from the bank, there was no sign of him. He had disappeared.

She sat down beside the fire and tried to think what she had done, to wonder *why* she had done it. She loved dogs. She couldn't understand what had come over her. He was starving! She had meat there ready and he would have come for it, but she had driven him away. She had driven him away twice now, the evening before with a branch flaming from the fire. He would not come again.

9

Warn Your Children!

Dr. Furness brought the others back twenty minutes later. Bron heard them talking as they came up from the road and felt suddenly and unaccountably shy. She ran to fetch *Warrior Scarlet* from her tent, and pretended to be reading it as they came into the camp.

Joe and Peter took the box of groceries that they were carrying between them into the store tent. Bron stood up.

'So you're another bookworm, are you?' said Dr. Furness, smiling at her. 'You and Margery make a good pair. I don't suppose you've missed this noisy crowd at all.'

He stayed for a short time, admiring their camp arrangements and the view, and then went down the hillside to his car. Five minutes later he was back again.

'Nearly forgot all about it,' he said cheerfully. 'The police have been patrolling the town with a loudspeaker van, saying "Warn your children!" And so I made a mental note to warn mine. Don't think I can have told your mother about it yet, either.'

'What, Dad?' asked Peter. 'Has somebody been dropping live explosives or dangerous drugs in the street? Or is there a lion at large?'

'Not a lion,' said his father, sitting on the bank to refill his pipe. 'An army dog. Alsatian. Jumped the train on Friday afternoon. Train was *en route* for Bristol, but made a special stop at Ludlow to pick up some vital hospital equipment. Dog sloped off. Only been seen once, since. Farmer saw it beyond Hopton Cangeford. It's muzzled, of course, so must be a bit peckish by now.'

He turned his back on them, to shelter the match flame from the wind.

'Oh, Uncle!' exclaimed Anne excitedly. 'We've seen it as well! It was here, last night, standing on that bank that you're sitting on. It's huge! I thought it was a wolf, because Bron was reading us a story with a wolf bit in it, and nobody believed that I'd seen it at all.'

'Did anyone else?' Dr. Furness looked doubtfully round at the others. He thought that Anne could quite easily have imagined it, knowing how nervous she was of the dark.

'No, nobody,' said Peter. 'She was moonstruck!'

Joe turned to Bron. 'Didn't you?' he asked. 'You ran straight up on to the bank.'

Bron stared at him and then at Anne. 'No,' she said.

Joe looked surprised. Anne looked cross.

'Well, I don't care if no one else *did* see it. I saw it. I know I did! It was grey, and I thought it was a wolf because alsatians are the same shape as wolves.'

'Hmn.' Dr. Furness looked at her thoughtfully. 'It is a grey dog. The police announcement said that it was.'

'But any reasonably light-coloured coat would look grey in moonlight,' pointed out Peter. 'Perhaps it was a sheep!'

His father frowned at him. 'Those army dogs are trained to be pretty savage, you know, and this particular one is even less reliable than most, because of partial deafness. It was being discharged from the army because of it. Whether Anne saw it last night or not, I want you to keep your eyes open. If it was beyond Hopton Cangeford on Saturday afternoon, it could well be in this area.'

'But it wouldn't attack a human, surely, Dad!' said
Margery. 'I suppose it could kill a lamb, though.'

'The point is that it can't kill anything until it rids itself
of the muzzle, and that therefore it might attack a man
in desperation if he had food with him.' Dr. Furness turned
to Bron. 'You have been alone up here all morning, Bronwen. Have you seen any large dog about, even at a distance?'

Bron didn't appear to hear what he asked her, so Margery
repeated the question. Bron frowned at no one in particular
and said shortly, 'No.'

He looked at her. The girl was pale and seemed a bit
miserable. He remembered that Margery had said she'd
stayed behind because of a headache, and hoped that she
wasn't sickening for anything.

'Well,' he said. 'It's time I wasn't here. Your mother will
be giving my dinner to Lucy if I don't get a move on. Give
us a ring in a day or two, and remember to keep a good
watch for that dog.'

They went down to the road with him and then hurried
back to Nordy Bank for their own dinner.

Low clouds crowded into the sky in the afternoon and
hid the hills. They decided that it was no use walking up to
Abdon Burf, as they had planned to do. In any case, by
the time they had cleared up after their meal it was rather late.

'It's a bit dismal, isn't it?' said Peter. 'If we finish the hut
off properly, we could sit in there this evening and probably
be much warmer than up on the top here.'

They agreed to do this and scattered along the side of the
hill, looking for more stones. The back wall of the hut was
complete, and the roof thatched with bracken between
hawthorn boughs. Joe sat in the ditch making a frame for
the door.

'How are you going to fix the door into the wall?' asked Margery, coming up to him. She held one end of a groundsheet, half filled with stones, and Bron held the other.

Joe said that he had no idea, but that she wasn't to tell Peter. 'He'll take this nice sitting-down job away from me, if you do,' he explained, 'and come and do it himself. As long as he thinks I know what I'm doing, he'll be quite happy to go on heaving stones up the hill.'

He looked so smug as he said this and pulled such a funny face afterwards that Margery couldn't stop giggling for a few moments. Looking up at the two of them, Joe was struck by the difference in their expressions. Bron looked most disagreeable; sulky and rather supercilious at the same time, as though she thought them both childish.

As the afternoon went on, everyone began to think the same, although no one said anything about it. Robin, who was always kindhearted, remembered that she had said she had a headache when they went into Ludlow without her, and tried to be extra friendly. Joe also thought that she wasn't very well. Anne and Peter were rather less charitable, and simply thought her irritable and unpleasant. Margery was puzzled and began to wonder if she had done something to offend her, because Bron snapped at her whenever she tried to cheer her up.

Bron was trying very hard not to. She saw Margery's face, reflecting the hurt of her snubs and sarcastic remarks, and was horrified by her own behaviour. She thought repeatedly of pleasant, ordinary things to say, but her tongue simply refused to say them. It was as if she were acting in a silent film, her own voice being shut off, to be instantly replaced by a dubbed voice, saying things with which she had no connexion, which she herself would never have said because she wasn't that sort of person. She wanted to explain this to Margery, or to anyone, but she couldn't. Alone in herself, Bron was feeling afraid.

At tea-time Peter asked Margery to go down with him to the farm to fetch some more water, and began to talk about Bron's bad temper as soon as they were out of hearing.

'What on earth did you have to invite *her* for?' he demanded. 'She goes about the whole time looking as though she's lost a shilling and found sixpence, as miserable as can be.'

'She's not usually at all like that. I've not often known her disagree with anyone before, let alone answer back in a temper.'

'That's just the trouble,' said Peter. 'She did at least argue a couple of days ago, and she did seem to know what she was talking about. Now almost all she says is "No", and scowls like a wild woman. That's just what she looks like, come to think of it: as though she'd like to lay about her with a stone axe!'

'Peter!' Margery was getting cross herself, especially so because she couldn't help agreeing with him and felt disloyal. 'What a thing to say! Don't be so ridiculous! She's usually just shy and a bit dreamy, but as nice as can be. I've never liked anybody as much as I like Bron. It's only since we came here that she's been different. It's the hill; it's changed her. It worries me.'

'Now *you're* being ridiculous! What influence could a hill have? The fact of the matter is, you don't know her properly, because you have only known her for a year, haven't you? She's probably got a split personality. She's schizophrenic, that's all. She's another Jekyll and Hyde!'

They finished by quarrelling heartily themselves, and carried the water back up to the camp in silence.

It was rather a quarrelsome evening altogether. They sat in the hut and were nicely out of the wind. Joe had built a rough fireplace just outside the door and they let the fire in the camp go out when they had lit another one there.

Robin had brought one of his geology books back with him from Bromfield, and tried to make Anne interested by showing her the photographs of fossils.

'Look at this smashing trilobite,' he said enthusiastically. 'I found one nearly as good as that, when we went to Millichope with Mr. Norton. You never know what you're going to pick up round here. That's what makes it so exciting.'

'Exciting!' Anne passed the book back to him. 'When do any of you find anything that's exciting? Really exciting, I mean, not just a bit of stone in the shape of a shell.'

'I found a prehistoric flint scraper that's in the museum now,' said Margery, proudly. 'It's a lovely black and amber one, and still quite sharp. When you hold it, you can feel where *their* fingers used to. It seems to settle itself naturally into the right position in your hand.'

Anne appeared quite unimpressed.

'Where did you find it?' asked Bron abruptly.

'On the little road back from Clun, by Pen-y-Cwm, below Black Hill.'

'The old Flint Trail ran there.' Bron was obviously speaking to herself.

'And did you see what Reynolds brought in a week or so back, from Newcastle-on-Clun?' Joe asked Peter, rather hurriedly, because he was obviously going to try to provoke Bron to argument again.

Peter nodded. 'Colin Reynolds, was it? I saw the axe head at the museum last week. It's a beauty.'

'How old is it?' said Anne, being interested now because Peter was. 'I still don't think I'd really call that exciting though, even if it were Roman.'

'It *feels* exciting in your hand,' said Bron, suddenly. 'Alive and powerful.'

'Yes.' Joe agreed with her. 'It had been cleaned before it was realized what it was, which really shouldn't be done, but I liked to see it like that. Nice and bright. Not at all as if it had been in existence for almost three thousand five hundred years.'

'It's a Bronze Age flat axe,' said Peter to Anne, because they hadn't told her yet. 'Mr. Norton dated it at about 1500 B.C.'

Anne opened her mouth to say 'How interesting!' without meaning it, but gave a small scream instead. The ground shivered as the dull thud of galloping hoofs came towards them along the side of the hill.

She was the only one who stayed in the hut. The others tumbled quickly out on to the bank, but the sound had swept past below them and they were too late to see anything.

'Blow!' said Robin. 'It's quite light still and we'd have seen them well if we'd been a bit quicker.'

'More coming,' said Peter.

A scattered bunch of ponies came fast towards them, but swerved down the hill-side and into the bracken.

'They're slowing up,' said Joe. 'Something must have startled them higher on the hill. Perhaps that army dog *is* round here somewhere.'

10

Abdon Burf

In the morning Arthur came up to the camp while they were eating breakfast. Both he and Edward had been working away from the house when Peter and Joe went down to fetch the milk and the day's water supply.

"Morning to you,' he said in his slow voice. 'I've just walked up here to see if you've made your plans for the day.'

'Not yet,' said Peter. 'We want to go up to look at Abdon Burf some time, but we're wondering what the weather's going to do.'

Arthur turned to look across Corvedale to the hills. 'It'll clear, I reckon. There's a good wind to get rid of the cloud, but maybe it'll not do it before midday.'

'Did you want us to help on a job?' asked Joe eagerly. He was used to working with his father in any spare time that he had and always began to feel rather fidgety after a week of absolute holiday.

'If you've the time to spare,' said Arthur. 'We bought a score of Hereford bullocks at the auction and want them in the bottom field by the brook. Hedges were safe enough before that great snowfall we had. Now there's several holes want filling in and some mending done on the rail fence along the top as well. The weight of drifts snapped the old posts like they were twigs.

'We're all behind with the sowing, as you'll know.' He nodded to Joe. 'The ground's only just dried out enough for us to get on it, so Ed and myself don't want to be stop-

gaps today. If you boys can manage it on your own, we can
stay with the barley. Be a great help.'

Finally, they all went down to work under Joe's direction,
except Bron. Peter had wanted Anne to stay at the camp, to
make an early dinner so that they would have a long afternoon, but she refused. She said that she was afraid of the
alsatian. Bron said that she preferred to stay on the hill, in
any case, and so they left her alone there for the third time.

They had all worked hard at gap-stopping and Bron had
the stew cooked early, so it was before one o'clock when
they set off.

They went up to the left of Clee Burf, over towards Five
Springs and the waist of the hill. The ground was rough,
very wet in places and patched with tangles of dead bracken
and gorse. Fortunately they all had Wellington boots on
and so missed the worst of the scratchiness, but even so
they had to keep their eyes on the ground ahead for some
time and watch where they were going. Consequently they
were surprised to find the ponies so near by.

A little herd of about fifteen were moving in a leisurely way
down towards the cleared grazing that lay along the Cockshut-
ford valley. The yearlings watched the children curiously
and with anxiety, but the old horses paid them no attention.

They stood still for a moment to watch them and after
the noise of their own movement had ceased, found a
surprising silence. There was the soft, flustery sound of the
wind in it, the occasional thud of a pony's stamping hoof,
the regular brisk tearing of grass, and sudden and far off
the bubbling, joyful cry of a curlew.

'Strange, isn't it?' said Joe. 'How some sounds only make
quiet seem quieter?'

They all nodded except Anne, who moved towards the

ponies in a cocksure way, holding her hand out and chirruping gaily. They glanced at her disdainfully, knowing that she had nothing for them, and drifted on evasively down the hill.

'Stupid creatures!' she said, rejoining the others. 'Even the worst ponies at my riding school are better than they are. Their heads are nearly as big as their shoulders and their coats are awful! They look absolutely moth-eaten.'

'So would you, if you'd been out all winter in that snow,' said Peter, turning uphill again. 'They're only shedding their winter coats.'

Five more ponies had been standing above them, waiting for them to move on, and now cantered away along the skyline, their manes and tails lifting in the wind, stepping high over the rough ground. Even Anne had to admit that they looked better in action, and that their squat sturdiness seemed suited to the strength of the hill behind them.

'Think how silly one of your scraggy riding-school ponies would look here,' pointed out Joe. 'It would have broken its leg in a week or died of pneumonia in a month.'

The sun struggled out into an acre of clear sky and they went on more cheerfully along the ridge.

They reached Abdon Burf with no further delay than the inevitable ones caused by Anne's inexperience. First she trod confidently into a pool of shallow-seeming bog water, and fell flat on her face when the black mud gave way gently beneath her and the water rose above her knees. Then she leapt screaming into a gorse bush because she thought that a black and twisted heather root which lay shining on the path was an adder.

After a little comfort from everyone, and a little sarcasm from Peter, she was reassured enough to go on to the top of the hill. Then they all sat quietly on the rough concrete

ledge at the bottom of the trig point, and looked at the view.

The four sides of it were surprisingly different. To the west it was a green view. The sweep of green hills was all that lay between them and the horizon of grey hills against grey sky. To the east, it was a dappled, varied view of grey and green, pink and brown. The woodlands were grey as yet, with only a thin green chiffon haze of breaking buds over them. The ploughed land was pink where it was freshly turned, paling to a soft brown as it lay, and the plain stretched away unbroken towards Bridgnorth and to Wolverhampton beyond it.

To the north crouched the Wrekin, the curve of its humped back and the smaller crest of the lowered head looking more like a sleeping dragon than a hill. To the south, back along the line of the Brown Clee, rose the wave-crest of the Titterstone Clee.

'This is the first time that I've been able to believe that this hill is forty feet higher than that one,' said Margery, pointing to it, 'but you do seem to look down on it a little from here. I suppose it's just the different shapes; this is such a round-shouldered, humpy hill that it looks lower than it really is.'

'In any case,' said Joe, 'this one has had its top taken off by the quarrying. It might have been a better shape before that.'

In the early springtime Abdon Burf still had a slightly sinister air about it. The black cushions of dead heather were interspersed with dark pools of stagnant bog-water. The overgrown mounds left by the old quarries made a moon landscape of what must have once been a smooth summit, and derelict buildings added to the gloom.

It was a relief to look outwards to the unspoilt hills, and they soon walked back again along the spine of the Brown Clee towards Clee Burf and the distinct, encircling fortifications of Nordy Bank.

As they walked down the slope from the main hill towards the camp, they spread out. Each picked his own way between the patches of bog and the old growth of tangled gorse and bracken—except Anne, who followed Peter.

When Joe saw the grey alsatian backing out from the store tent, he shouted and began to run. Bron, who was some way in front of the others, shouted, too, and ran so fast that even Peter couldn't catch up with her. Anne stayed where she was.

The dog had gone when they got there, of course. The loaf of bread that he had been dragging with him lay just beyond the mouth of the tent.

'No teeth marks,' pointed out Joe. 'He must have clawed it out of the box. Poor creature must still be muzzled, and pretty desperate by now.'

'Weak, too,' said Peter. 'Maybe he's lying up somewhere below us in the bracken. I think that we ought to beat our way through it before dusk. Where are those two girls?'

Anne was coming slowly down the hill. Bron was piling branches on to the fire and Peter went straight across to take off again all those which had not caught light.

'It's quite warm now,' he said, when she frowned at him, 'and we've not much wood left anyway. There's no need for a huge fire like that.'

'They are afraid of fire,' she said, and turned away from him to look down the hill-side.

They searched the bracken thoroughly. Even Anne was persuaded to walk in the middle of the line, but they saw no further sign of the alsatian. Then Joe suggested that Bron, Anne, and Margery should sleep in the hut until they heard that the dog had been caught. Peter thought this a good idea, and informed Robin that he must sleep in the hut, too.

'Well, I'm not going to, so there,' said Robin firmly. 'Just because I'm the youngest, you always treat me as though I'm still a baby.'

During the ensuing noisy argument, Margery went to sit beside Bron on the bank. She hesitated for a while before speaking, because she didn't quite know how to say what she wanted to. In the end she simply asked a straight-forward question.

'Why did you keep shouting "Wolf!" when we saw the army dog this afternoon?'

'Did I?' asked Bron, without looking at her.

'Yes, you did. And you shouted it that first time when you and Anne saw him on the bank. You did see him then, didn't you?'

Bron stared at her, a most strange and dreadfully sorrowful expression on her face. She moved suddenly on the bank, almost a convulsive movement, her fingers clutching the grass, her breath catching in her throat. Margery leaned forward quickly and touched her arm.

'Bron?' she said anxiously. 'Are you all right?'

After a short pause, Bron turned to her. 'Yes,' she said, but without conviction, and tried to smile.

Then Margery saw from her eyes that now she was really afraid.

11

Let the Dog Starve!

The wind blew gustily for most of the night, but then dropped slowly away down the hill-side. By morning the clouds had gathered themselves together again and shut Corvedale in under a low grey ceiling.

'How miserable!' said Margery, as they sat eating breakfast in silence. 'It's like being in a room with no windows, sort of airless.'

'Yes,' said Peter. 'I don't feel much like tramping down to the village, but I suppose I'd better. Are there any groceries to get, besides bread, while I'm there?'

'What are you going for, then, if it's not for food?' asked Anne.

'To telephone, of course. Since we've got to let them know at Bromfield that we're still alive in any case, I'll just phone there, I think. Then Dad can ring up the police or the army, or whoever's pidgin it is, and tell them that the dog was definitely here last night.'

'Be miles away by now,' said Joe. 'Who's going down for the milk while you go to the village?'

'Bron and I'll go, for a change,' said Margery. 'Then you can patch that cracky bit of the hut roof where the wind blew in all last night. Anne will show you where it is.'

When they walked round the corner of the farmhouse into the yard, Margery and Bron were practically pushed over by five large, lively, and welcoming lambs, all convinced that they had come to feed them. So they waded along to the kitchen door with some difficulty, knee-deep in woolly escort.

Edward saved them by sending Trix, the old dog, to hustle the lambs back into the orchard, and then returned to his cup of strong orange-coloured tea.

'They'm the old tiddlings,' he said in explanation.

Margery looked puzzled, so Bron explained further, 'Cade lambs. Motherless.' Margery nodded.

While they measured out the milk from the small churn in the corner, Edward watched them, but made no attempt at conversation. He usually left all the talking to Arthur. This morning Arthur was in Ludlow.

Margery roused him from his silence when she told him about their encounter with the army dog on the previous evening.

'I expect policemen or soldiers will come up here to look for him now. I do hope they manage to catch him, for his own sake.'

Edward poured himself a second cup of thick tea. 'Let the dog starve!' he said.

'Why ever do you say that?' said Margery indignantly. 'Somebody's got to help him.'

'Got nothing against the dog.' Edward rinsed his tea cup under the tap and put it upside down on the draining-board. 'Save themselves a deal of trouble if they leave it be for another couple of days, that's all. Too much cover here to catch it by chasing it about. Let it starve a bit longer, and it'll come and give itself up. No question of that.'

He went out. Margery continued to talk excitedly about joining in the search for the alsatian, while Bron filled a bucket with water to take back to Nordy Bank and listened to her in silence.

Anne had shown Joe which corner of the hut roof needed reinforcing with more bracken. Now she was sitting on the bank above it, watching him and Robin at work, and peeling the potatoes.

She saw nothing strange in the behaviour of the sheep farther down the hill-side. They were running to gather themselves together into a little flock, holding their heads high and calling anxiously to their lambs. Joe, however, stopped talking to Robin to listen. Then he climbed slowly up the bank to Anne.

'Don't move,' he said. 'I'm wondering what all this baaing is about. Something's worrying the ewes.'

Robin joined them and they sat in silence, staring down at the sheep.

'I see him,' said Joe suddenly. 'The alsatian. He's about ten feet directly in front of that small thorn bush. Shall we have a go at catching him, Robin?'

Robin nodded excitedly.

'Well, we'll have to take it slowly. No good frightening him again. You'd better stay here, Anne, hadn't you? We'll go into the store tent first to grab a piece of meat each, Robin, then you go towards the farm and I'll go the other way. Go down below the bracken line first and then work up again behind him. All right? If you manage to get near enough, just talk to him quietly and let him get a whiff of the meat, then sit down. I think that he may come. Must be in a poor way by now.'

They went down behind the bank, leaving Anne sitting alone and already nervous. She saw them both moving slowly down the hill-side, making a wide detour round the little thorn tree until they were quite a way below it. Then the dog stood up.

Anne scrambled to her feet, clutching at her skirt in fear.

The alsatian saw her and moved hesitantly forward. Anne was afraid even of small dogs—this huge grey-brindled creature appeared as savage and menacing as a wolf to her. She looked wildly around for a weapon of defence, saw only the potatoes lying on the bank, and stooped swiftly to pick them up.

The alsatian stood still, and snarled. Anne screamed, threw at him all the potatoes that she could lay her hands on, leapt down into the ditch, scrambled into the hut, and jammed the door shut.

The dog swung round and began to run, found Robin almost directly behind him, knocked him down in passing and bounded away across the bracken, the terrified sheep scattering in all directions.

When Margery and Bron returned they found Robin and Joe, weak with laughter, trying to persuade Anne to come out from the hut.

'It's just like the three little pigs,' giggled Robin, after Joe had explained what had happened. 'Come on out, Anne, you silly piggy! Or I'll huff and I'll puff and I'll blow your house down!'

Margery frowned at him. 'Don't be unkind, Robin. Do come out now, Anne. It really is quite safe.'

After several moments of such reassurance, she did so. When Peter arrived back in the camp shortly afterwards, he found all three girls peeling the few potatoes that had been left on the bank, while Joe and Robin walked about in the bracken a little farther down the hill. They were looking, not very hopefully, for those thrown by Anne at the alsatian. They found three.

While they ate their dinner Peter heard the two versions of what had happened. Anne's was by far the more exciting.

Joe said simply that the dog seemed so starved that there was no fight left in him. The poor creature was as thin as a rake.

'Poor creature!' exclaimed Anne indignantly. 'How can you say that? He was coming for me, snarling, until I threw the potatoes, and then he attacked Robin.'

'He didn't attack me. He only tripped over me in passing!' pointed out Robin. 'I was right behind him.'

'Well, I still think he's dangerous, whatever you may say. I don't think that we ought to stay here any longer. It's not safe.'

'And where do you suggest that we move to?' Peter was amused. 'Would the race-course at Bromfield be safe enough for you? Or is that still too far from the house?'

Bron laughed loudly, in a rather unkind way. 'The camp must stay on the hill,' she said. 'There is no need to be so much afraid of one wolf!'

Peter, Joe, and Robin all laughed, too, thinking that she was teasing Anne. Margery knew Bron better than that. She was so shy and sensitive to hurt herself that she rarely teased others. Looking across at her now, Margery felt again the strangeness of Bron's changed behaviour. It would be impossible to convince Peter of it and of no use to take the subject up again with him, but on the hill she had become a dreadfully different person.

So Margery surprised everyone by agreeing with Anne. 'I think that we ought to move, too. We've explored the hill now, and perhaps Arthur will let us camp down at the bottom of the big meadow by the Clee Brook.'

Robin looked interested. Joe shrugged, because he didn't mind where they went. Anne was pleased, and smiled.

Bron looked bewildered. 'The camp must stay on the hill,' she repeated, as though trying to convince herself of it.

Peter closed the argument. 'Well, we can't move it tomorrow, and if we don't move it tomorrow it's not worth the bother, because we'll be going home soon after that, in any case.'

'Why can't we move it tomorrow?' Anne was sliding into a sulk.

'Because we have to go into Bromfield in the morning, that's why. Your parents are calling in on their way back to Bristol, so we've to go for dinner *and* tea. Ma told me when I phoned them.'

Anne was much cheered by this. 'But how are we going to get there?'

'I've no idea,' said Peter, 'but I'll ask Arthur this evening when I go down for more water. He may know of someone who's going into Ludlow.'

While Peter and Joe were down at the farm, the others scattered along the roadside hedges, looking for firewood. Margery found herself alone with Bron and tried to cheer her up by telling her about Lucy's puppies.

'We can stay with the dogs for most of the day tomorrow,' she said, knowing how much Bron disliked meeting strangers. 'We'll take them out for their walks, shall we? If we can manage two each, we can get through them all in two journeys and go quite a long way.'

'I'm not coming,' said Bron abruptly.

Margery stood still and stared at her. 'Look, I do wish you'd tell me what's the matter! Something must be. Do you feel ill, or anything, Bron?'

She shook her head. 'I'm all right.'

'But you've changed! Don't you feel any different yourself? I can't understand it, but I'm sure it's to do with this hill, with Nordy Bank. You *must* come down to Bromfield with us tomorrow. I shan't let you stay here alone again.'

For a moment Bron looked at her, an almost terrified expression on her face, seeming not to know what to say in reply. Then she turned quickly away, saying loudly, 'Leave me alone! Mind your own business.'

Margery followed her up to Nordy Bank in silence.

12

Alone on the Hill

No one made any comment when Bron said before break-fast that she was not going with them into Bromfield. Margery realized that it was of no use to argue further about it, but was very much relieved when Joe said that he would prefer to stay as well.

'I'm not a great one for family parties,' he explained. 'I'd rather roam about on the hill for a bit and maybe do a few odd jobs for Arthur.'

He went down with Peter to fetch the water and the milk, and to ask about this. Peter was asking for advice about possible transport into Ludlow.

When they came back into the camp they were both smiling.

'Well, we've arranged a lift in,' said Peter, 'with Edward. He's leaving at ten-thirty, so we must be down at the gate by then. He's going to take his girlfriend out for a ride because it's early closing and she has the afternoon off.'

Then the others began to laugh a little, too, at the thought of Edward having a girlfriend. It somehow didn't seem to fit in with what they knew of his character.

'I wonder who does the talking?' said Margery. 'I'm sure I've never heard him speak more than three times.'

But when the old black Austin drew up at the field gate at half past ten, Edward looked a different man. Everything about him shone, his face, his hair, his shoes, and even his suit, although this was through hard wear and so more by accident than design.

After the others had gone, Bron sat in the doorway of the hut until it was time to get the dinner ready, apparently reading Robin's book about fossils. Joe went to help Arthur finish some late corn drilling.

As he crossed the road to return to the camp, at twelve o'clock, a Land Rover drew up to turn into Arthur's gateway. The driver was the father of one of Joe's friends, and he stood in the road for several minutes, talking to him. Then he went on quickly up to Nordy Bank.

'Bron,' he said, standing on the bank above the hut to look down at her, 'we've an invitation for dinner, if you'd like to come. I don't suppose you know Dick Minton; he lives on a farm near Abdon. I've just met his Dad and he's asked us over.'

'I'd rather stay here. I'll be all right.' Bron looked even more unfriendly than usual.

Joe hesitated. 'Are you sure you won't mind being on your own? The alsatian might come back.'

'No. I like being on my own.'

She went on reading. Joe stared down at her for a moment, puzzled, then shrugged his shoulders, said 'Good-bye', and went quickly down to the road again.

When he had gone Bron put the book down. She sat quite still, looking at nothing in particular, feeling miserable, confused, and frightened.

Each day it grew stronger, the shadow within herself. Since that first time of being alone on Nordy Bank, when she had felt uneasily that she was somehow *not* alone, its presence had been with her. At first, she had thought the strangeness might be the beginnings of 'flu, or unexpected homesickness. Now that she had realized the power of it she could not imagine how she could escape.

At half past twelve Bron roused herself and went up into the camp. The edge of the wind was cold and everything in the view drab and unfriendly; grey sky, grey hills, grey grass. She wished that she had gone with Joe.

It seemed too much bother to cook a proper meal, or even to boil an egg. Anyway, the fire was out. She squatted in the store tent to see what was there, and took back bread, butter, and cheese to the fireside. Then she went to collect some chocolate wholemeal biscuits, two bananas and an apple. She was half-way back before she looked up. She stopped suddenly. The alsatian stopped suddenly.

He had been almost crawling down from the bank, his body low to the ground, the belly and the beautiful tail brushing the grass. Now the pricked ears were laid back, the tail curled between the hind legs, in supplication.

Bron stood still. She was prepared this time for the conflict of emotions: the rush of warm pity and the strong urge to help the starving animal, which was crossed by the fearfully cold lust to drive it away or to kill it, and backed by a strange shadow of terror in her mind. She moved quietly forward.

Anne's mother was a pretty woman, but comfortably fat, with chubby cheeks and dimples at the knuckle end of each pudgy finger. She kissed the children as they came in, uttering all the usual joyful little cries: 'My, *how* you've grown, Peter!'; 'You're more like your Dad than ever, Margery!'; 'There, Robin, so you're not a baby now!' Peter was extremely pleased that Joe had stayed at the camp.

Mr. Turner, Anne's father, removed his pipe just long

N.B.—G

enough to say, 'Hello. Glad to see you', before puffing placidly at it again with little popping noises.

Anne began talking as soon as she entered the front door and talked without stopping for a full quarter of an hour.

'Honestly, you never saw anything like it! A *huge* dog it was, more like a wolf really to look at, a great big grey thing. The first time I saw it, at night, its eyes were shining

red in the firelight and it just terrified me. Can you imagine it, Mummy? Bron said she never saw it, but I know she did. It was huge. You couldn't miss it. Peter kept laughing at me, didn't you, Peter? But I was right.'

One by one, Peter, Margery, and Robin drifted away. They decided that there was time to take the dogs for a walk before dinner, and went off with two each, leaving the remaining two sitting doleful and disconsolate by the door of the pen.

After dinner, Robin was captured by his mother and made to be polite to the visitors in the garden. Peter escaped, and took the two now jubilant dalmatians for *their* walk. Margery followed her father from the room and slid round the surgery door so softly that he didn't know she was there.

'Well,' he said to himself, walking across to his desk. 'Now for a bit of peace and quiet. What a pair of rattles!'

Margery laughed and he turned, smiled at her, then pointed to the door.

'You, too! Out! I'm busy. Form-filling.'

He picked up his pen, but Margery remained standing in front of him.

'Please, I'm here in a professional capacity. I want some advice.'

'Who's sick, then? None of you here. Is it Bronwen? Thought she might be sickening for something last time I saw her. Where's the rash and how long has she had it? Or is it a lump?'

'It's neither. It's in her head.'

'Pain? A headache? You should have made her come with you.'

'No. It's nothing like that. It's just that since we've been in the camp, she's changed completely. *I* think that the spirit of the hill has possessed her or something, and it's getting worse now because she's beginning to be very frightened of it herself. She says that she isn't, but I know she is.'

'Balderdash!' Dr. Furness tipped his chair back to reach for a pile of record cards. 'Cuckoo! What do you mean, changed?'

'Well, she began by being terribly aggressive and argumentative, but now she's just shut up inside herself. She knew all sorts of things about the fortress on Nordy Bank, and how the Iron Age people lived, and she kept calling that army dog a wolf. She went for it with a blazing branch from the fire, the first time she saw it.'

'Then she's lucky it didn't attack her! Even with a muzzle on.' He looked amused.

'I know you don't believe me, but just *suppose* that she were possessed by the spirit of an Iron Age woman or something like that, what ought I to do? She's getting worse, really she is!'

'Most probably homesickness, or an upset stomach! Still, I'll answer your supposition, to be rid of you. Now, I definitely do not admit that anyone can be possessed by the spirit of a dead person—least of all a soul from a body dead for two thousand five hundred years! But, supposing your supposition to be a fact, surely the logical action would be to remove her as far as possible from the scene of this so-called possession. In other words, strike camp and go to stay in Birmingham. That should shake any poor Iron Age soul to its rock bottom! Now toddle off, Margery. I'm really busy.'

Margery thanked him, and went.

As Joe walked up to the camp from the road, he saw Bron's head above the top of the bank, as if she were watching for him. She waved, and then ran down the hill to meet him.

'Hello,' she called. 'Hasn't it been a lovely afternoon? Have you enjoyed your visit?'

Joe stood still and stared at her. She looked a different person altogether from the sullen girl he had left earlier in the day. She was smiling, and looked somehow tremendously excited.

Bron didn't wait for his answer, but went on, 'I've a surprise for you, but you must walk very quietly into the camp or the surprise might not like it! I don't quite know what's going to happen!'

Joe understood her when he saw the alsatian, lying down beside the fire, but with his head turned suspiciously in their direction.

'He's rather deaf,' said Bron softly. 'Do you remember Dr. Furness telling us? I speak very slowly to him and try not to move too suddenly. I do hope he's going to be all right with you.'

The dog stood up as she spoke, began to move towards them, and snarled.

'Down, Griff!' Bron spoke clearly but not too loudly, and made a firm downward gesture with her arm as she did so. He stopped, reluctantly, and slowly sat down. Bron sat beside him. The alsatian moved closer to her and leaned his shoulder against her leg. He watched Joe carefully.

Joe sat down himself, speechless with astonishment. He saw that the unbuckled muzzle lay beside the fire, together with an empty tin which had held corned beef. A thick leather strap was still attached to the dog's collar.

'However did you do it?' said Joe. 'And why do you call him Griff?'

'I don't really know *how* I did it. He came over the bank as I was getting my dinner ready, soon after you'd gone. I suppose he'd been lurking in the bracken and then smelt the cheese or something. Anyway, I held some out to him and he came up to me very slowly. He kept snarling and drawing back, but whining with hunger all at the same time somehow.

'I daren't try to unbuckle the muzzle until I'd given him some food. I thought he might attack me. So I broke up the cheese and fed it to him through it. He swallowed the pieces whole with the most dreadful sort of snapping, snarling noise. Then I took the muzzle from him and gave him a drink, although he didn't seem so very thirsty. I suppose he'd been able to suck some water up from the streams. After that I opened the biggest tin of corned beef we had and mixed it with some crumbled biscuit. When he'd eaten that, he lay down beside the fireplace and went to sleep.

'I don't know why I call him Griff, though. It just came to me! It seems to suit him, doesn't it?'

'Yes,' said Joe. 'Suits him well.'

When they heard a car stop in the road below them and the door slam, Joe peered over the bank. 'The others. Anne's parents as well, by the look of things. Come to see the camp, I suppose. What will you do?'

Bron stood up and the alsatian with her. She held the end of the strap.

'Better not to confuse him with a lot of hullabaloo. I'll go round quickly to the left and then down, so that I should be out of sight by the time they get up here. Tell them I've gone for a walk.'

Anne's parents admired everything: the view, the camp site, the fireplace, and the hut. They were introduced to Joe and thought him a nice quiet boy. Peter and Margery wondered what was the matter with him.

He remained seated beside the fireplace even while he was introduced, and then said hardly another word, simply staring pensively at the fire. He was sitting on the leather muzzle of an army dog.

13

I Have Him Safe

When they were back in the camp, after seeing their visitors away, Margery went straight up to Joe, who still remained seated beside the fire.

'Where *is* Bron? When did she go for this walk? I know that something's happened because I can feel it in the air. And what do you think you're doing, sitting there grinning like a silly Cheshire cat?'

Joe shook his head and stayed where he was to annoy her. 'All in good time! I dare say Bron will come back when she feels like it and then she'll tell you herself. You must just wait and see.'

Margery sat on the bank to watch for her, and didn't have long to wait.

Bron's exit with Griff had been rather hurried. Her entrance now was dramatic and well-timed.

They all stood in astonished silence as she came quickly across the head of Nordy Bank towards them, the alsatian moving beside her at a slow, smooth trot.

'Isn't he beautiful?' she called. 'He's not at all fierce, Anne. There's no need to be frightened.'

Her excitement and happiness showed plainly in her face.

They soon found, however, that Griff reserved his friendship and his obedience only for Bron. While the others made no move to touch him, he treated them with indifference. But if anyone came too near or put out a hand towards him, he snarled, at first only silently, drawing his lips back over his teeth, and then angrily if they persisted, the deep growling note rising steadily.

While they ate their supper they argued about whether or not there was any chance of Bron's being allowed by the army to keep him.

'After all, they did say that he was being discharged because of his deafness,' said Bron hopefully. 'They must mean to give him to *somebody*.'

'Yes,' agreed Peter, 'but I shouldn't set your heart on it. After all, alsatians are worth quite a lot of money and I expect they'll want to sell him and not give him away.'

Margery said nothing, because she thought herself that more opposition was likely from Mrs. Owen than from the army. Moving from one flat to another as regularly as the family did made the keeping of any sort of dog difficult. Such a large dog as the alsatian would be impossible. There would be no room for him, even if the owner of the flat agreed to his being kept, which would be unlikely. In any case, Mrs. Owen was not particularly fond of dogs.

As Margery sat watching the others and worrying about this, she suddenly realized what was different about Bron. She was herself again. Not quite as she had been before—happier at the moment, because she had Griff, and more confident—but definitely herself again. She was listening to Robin when no one else was bothering to, smiling and looking interested about some idea he was explaining. Bron always had been a *listener*, before.

Supper seemed to have spread itself over a longer time than was usual, and when they had finished they mostly felt like going to bed. When Anne thought about it, she realized that she was expected to sleep within six feet of a very large, hostile, and ferocious army dog of unpredictable behaviour. She was horrified.

'You must tie him up somewhere,' she insisted, 'or shut him up, down at the farm. He's dangerous!'

'No. He'll be all right with me,' said Bron. 'I have him safe. Don't worry about him, Anne; I'm sure he won't attack you.'

'Unless Anne attacks him first!' added Peter sarcastically.

Finally it was decided that Bron should sleep in the hut and Margery insisted on sleeping there with her.

'Just to be on the safe side,' she explained, 'although I'm sure he'll be quiet. It's strange, how all dogs seem to trust you on sight.'

'Well, I also gave him half a pound of cheese, opened a tin of corned beef for him, and have fed him twice since then,' said Bron modestly. 'That does help!'

The hut was long enough to allow Bron and Margery's sleeping places to be well spaced from each other, so that Griff would be unlikely to take exception to Margery's presence in the middle of the night.

They talked for a long time. Bron was worried when she heard of Margery's talk with Dr. Furness, in case he asked her the reason for her changed behaviour when he saw her again. She didn't think that she wanted to explain to anyone what she had felt. She had been trying not to admit to herself the possibility of some other person having directed her thoughts and actions since they came to Nordy Bank. If she only talked about it to Margery, then surely even that would make it more real to her? It would be less easy to forget.

But suddenly she found herself wanting and needing to bring it out into the open for this one time, to talk about it, come to some conclusion about it, and so strip it of its fearful quality for good and all. It wouldn't matter then if she did *not* forget.

She stroked Griff's head to reassure herself. He moved contentedly under her hand and sighed so heavily that Margery laughed.

'It sounds almost as though there are three people in this hut!'

'Not now,' said Bron, 'although I think that there might have been, before.' And after a short silence, 'Do you mind if I tell you about it, Marge?'

'I wish you would. I know something very strange happened to you when we came here. No one felt it but me, because no one really knew you but me. Anyway it's gone now, whatever it was, hasn't it?'

'Yes. It's gone now. I can't understand it, really. I seemed to have a memory that wasn't mine and something in my body that wasn't me, and then today, when Griff came, it was more than that.' Bron was quiet for some time.

'How, more than that?' asked Margery encouragingly.

'I'm trying to think how to say it, because it might all have been in my imagination. Only really, I know it wasn't.

'I'd driven Griff away twice before: the first time when Anne saw him, and the second time when he came to me begging for food, while you'd all gone to see Lucy's puppies. I didn't *want* to drive him away, but something just seemed to make me. It was the same today. As soon as I saw him, I had the impulse to do it. Well, I sort of realized that it was coming, this time, and managed to stop it.'

She was silent again, until Margery said, 'Was that all?'

'No. Worse than that. After I'd taken his muzzle off and fed him, he lay down beside the fireplace and went to sleep. I suppose he'd been too hungry to sleep much before. I was sitting just behind him. Then, almost before I knew what it was doing, my right hand picked up one of those big corner stones from the hearth and swung it up into the air, above his head. It would have killed him. I knew that it was going to.

'Of course it was *my* hand, on the end of *my* arm, but it didn't seem to belong to me at all. It was doing what somebody else wanted it to, and not me. It was a most peculiar feeling, but I wasn't at all frightened—I was just angry. I grabbed the stone with my left hand and threw it hard down the bank, and then Griff woke up. He came and tucked his head under my arm; you know how dogs do, when they are feeling very affectionate. Well, I suddenly felt quite different. Really alone on the hill for the first time. That's all.

'Don't let's talk about it any more, though, Marge. I'm beginning to forget already. I'm glad I've been able to tell you. I wanted to.'

In a few minutes Bron was asleep, but Margery lay awake for a long time, trying to understand and not succeeding.

They woke in the morning to find Nordy Bank an island in a sea of mist. While they were having breakfast this thickened into a grey and depressing drizzle of rain, and when Joe went down for the day's milk both the B.B.C. and Arthur forecast that no improvement was likely.

Peter put into words what they were all thinking when he suggested that they strike camp and return to Bromfield.

'It was only fixed for a couple of days more, anyway,' he said. 'There's no point in hanging about up here catching pneumonia. We can sleep in our tent on the lawn, Joe, then there'll be room for the others in the house.'

'We would have to go into Ludlow in any case,' pointed out Margery, 'to do something about Griff.'

Peter and Joe went down to the village immediately after breakfast, to phone Bromfield and find out whether any transport would be available to take them home.

While they were gone Anne and Margery packed the remaining food and the kitchen equipment into boxes, Robin filled up the drains they had made beside the tents, and Bron began to pick the worst of the mud gently from Griff's rough coat. When they had finished, the others sat on the bank to watch her.

'I wish that I *wasn't* afraid of dogs,' remarked Anne sadly. 'But I always have been. They don't like me, either. Most of them growl if I try to make myself stroke them.'

'That's only because they know you're frightened,' said Bron, smiling sympathetically. 'Then it makes them nervous, too.'

'We're all afraid of *him*!' Margery pointed at Griff, who growled softly because of the sudden, threatening gesture. 'So don't let that worry you. But there's absolutely no need to be frightened of Lucy. She'd sooner bite herself than bite a human being!'

'Yes, I know there's no *need*,' explained Anne, 'but I just can't help it. I do try.'

'Everybody's frightened of something,' said Robin, in a helpful way. 'I'm frightened of going to the dentist, and *that's* silly.'

'And I'm frightened of balls,' said Margery, 'particularly hockey balls. And that's sillier still.'

'And I'm frightened of people,' said Bron, stroking Griff's head, 'and that's silliest of all.'

Dr. Furness said that he would just have time to fetch them that afternoon, but that they must be absolutely ready and waiting by the roadside at one-thirty.

Since half the party were born organizers, this was done with twenty minutes to spare and they spent them in Arthur's kitchen. Bron sat on the doorstep holding Griff's

lead, so that he could lie in the yard outside and not be surrounded by people. He was still very nervous.

'Good thing you've got him,' said Arthur. 'Poor animal. Good thing Edward's out, too, and both the dogs with him. Might have been a bit of trouble. No wonder he's on edge, is there? Being half deaf like he is, as well as in strange surroundings.'

'I've always thought it must be worse to be half deaf than completely deaf, in a way,' said Margery. 'You'd never quite know which direction a noise was coming from, whereas if you were really deaf you'd not hear it at all.'

When they heard the shooting-brake stop in the road they hurried out to it.

Dr. Furness admired Griff, but wisely did not try to stroke him.

'Well, here's a problem, Arthur!' he exclaimed. 'How to fit six large children, one large dog, and four tents into a non-elastic-sided shooting-brake! Not to mention the clothes and the cooking pots, and the fact that the large dog has a rather ferocious disposition.'

'I think I'll put his muzzle on again, shall I?' suggested Bron. 'To avoid accidents. I don't suppose he minds it, because I think that army dogs always do have them on for travelling. I saw about five of them once on Leicester station.'

'Good idea,' said Dr. Furness. 'Well, Peter, will it have to be done in two journeys? If so, it's going to be awkward, because I've only time to make this one before about nine-thirty this evening.'

'Not at all, Doc,' said Peter airily. 'Didn't you read about the two thousand university undergrads. who all got into a telephone box? There'll be plenty of room!'

'I hardly think that two thousand can be the correct figure,' said his father, 'but sort yourselves out at top speed. I've got an appointment.'

Peter grabbed the keys from the ignition and opened the tail doors, stood by them and began to shout for the things he wanted. The others formed a luggage-chain from the heap by the roadside to pass them to him as quickly as possible.

The fifth thing he called for, after the tents, was Robin who, despite protests, was packed in with the other things behind the back seat, and the doors closed on him. He peered at them indignantly through the rear window.

'Mind you lock those doors,' said Dr. Furness. 'Your mother and I would miss him, even if you wouldn't.'

The others squashed into the back seat, Margery on Peter's lap and Anne on Joe's, while Bron sat in comfort beside the driver, with Griff on the floor between her knees. Apart from jumping nervously when the car started, he behaved very well.

They thanked Arthur and waved good-bye to him, and all tried to catch a last glimpse of Nordy Bank as the car moved away. Robin had the best view, and saw the banks stand out clearly against the sky for a moment, before they merged into the background of green-brown hill-side. As the car went down towards Corvedale the long shape of the hill seemed to gather itself together and draw the rain-clouds round it for privacy.

Dr. Furness turned to Bron and said cheerfully, 'How are you now, then? Back to normal?'

She nodded and began to blush, and said, to change the subject, 'You've turned the wrong way. Aren't we going to Stoke St. Milborough?'

'Not today. It's rather quicker to cut across to Stanton Lacy.'

He drove as fast as was safe on the narrow, twisting roads, brushing between high banks starred with primroses and hazy with dog violets almost as big as pansies. Occasional groups of pale ladysmocks crowded the ditches, made more ethereal by the gaudy golden glow of the kingcups beneath them. A few early cowslips stood in the bright spring grass.

They were soon home. Mrs. Furness was full of enthusiasm over Griff, hopeful about the army's allowing Bron to keep him, and that his price would be within her reach.

'A good alsatian *is* worth a lot of money, it's true,' she said, 'but I don't think that he would do well as a show dog. His coat is too pale for one thing, and the angle of his back legs is wrong. The line of his back and tail should slope more, and also he stands too tall. All that will take a fair fraction from his value. He's beautiful, all the same.'

Bron couldn't help contrasting Mrs. Furness's reaction with the attitude which she was sure her mother would take. She would see Griff only as a very large dog, likely to shed hair on the furniture, and to bring mud into the house, and with a thoroughly untrustworthy disposition.

14

Quite Out of the Question!

Bron slept in Peter's room that night, because Anne was in the spare bedroom. Peter and Joe had put up their tent on the back lawn, watched closely by the dalmatians. Joe had felt something or someone looking at him, through his back, and had turned round to see eight spotted faces peering earnestly at him through the wire of the pens. He had light-heartedly suggested to Peter that they took their sleeping bags in and shared the dogs' communal sleeping-bench, to save the bother of putting up the tent, but Peter thought that although the dogs would probably like that, he probably would not.

Because she was in a strange bed, Bron was sleeping only in patches of the night. She was worried, too. Although she felt confident, for no reason, that the R.A.V.C. authority would allow her to keep Griff, she couldn't feel the same confidence in her mother. What made it worse was the fact that she could quite understand her mother's reasons.

She began to picture the house that would be perfect for them all—near a small town, with neighbours for her mother; a garage for her father, so that he wouldn't have to walk half a mile each morning before he even reached the car; a large garden for herself, so that she could keep Griff. This was a favourite pastime of hers and she went to sleep while she was doing it.

She woke again in the early hours of the morning and lay listening to the conversation of two cats in the road, carried out at first in thin plaintive voices like disgruntled fairies. When these rose to curdled howls and banshee wails, Griff woke too, and growled a little. Bron leaned from the bed to reassure him and felt the risen hair on his neck flattening beneath her hand. He nudged her arm with his nose and settled down again, and when Bron fell asleep a few minutes afterwards she slept until the morning.

Lucy's box of puppies was in the dining-room and the children were able to watch their scramblings while they had breakfast. Margery was very upset when Mrs. Furness suggested that it would be much better to have the smallest one put to sleep while it was still young.

'He's such a tiny thing,' she said, 'and such a very odd shape. He's sure to have spots in all the wrong places. You'll never find a buyer for him.'

'Well,' said Margery, making a sudden decision. 'He's not for sale then. I'm keeping him myself!'

'Do you remember,' remarked Dr. Furness suddenly, from behind his newspaper, 'what I said when you were allowed to keep Lucy?'

Margery said nothing.

'Then I'll repeat it. *No* more dogs. Nine spotted dogs are quite enough! You must do as your mother thinks best.'

Margery looked hopelessly at him and then went rather quickly to squat beside the box and stroke Lucy's head.

There was an awkward silence at the table, broken by Joe saying apologetically, 'I'd have him with pleasure, but we've three collies already and I don't somehow think he'd fit in.'

Margery said, 'It doesn't matter,' in a stiff voice which showed how much it did.

Anne took a piece of toast from the rack and began to

spread marmalade on to it, forgetting about butter. 'Could I have him, Margery?' she said, suddenly feeling very shy. 'I'm sure that Mummy would let me.'

Dr. Furness lowered the newspaper. Anne began to eat her toast, crunching into a sudden complete silence.

Mrs. Furness broke it. 'That's really kind of you, Anne,' she said, 'but are you sure? Don't be considerate for Margery's happiness at the expense of your own, now. I know that you're not fond of dogs.'

'But don't you see, Mummy?' said Margery, excitedly, standing up with the smallest puppy in her hand. 'This isn't a dog!'

'What is it then?' said Peter. 'A cabbage plant?'

'It's only the *beginning* of a dog.' Bron smiled broadly at Anne. 'By the time he's grown up to be one, Anne won't be thinking of him as a dog to be afraid of. He'll just be Toby by then, or Rex, or whatever else she decides to call him.'

'Toby or Rex!' exclaimed Robin in disgust. 'She can't give a dalmatian a name like that! She should call him Spotted Dick.'

Everyone laughed, relieved that the impending tragedy had been so happily averted.

'Be more subtle to call him Pudding,' remarked Peter.

Anne considered this. 'Yes, it would,' she said, 'but it's too undignified for a dalmatian, is Pudding. Dick's a good name.'

Breakfast was finished quickly, everyone suddenly in good spirits and being especially agreeable to Anne. Afterwards, she wrote a long letter home to her parents in Bristol, and Bron and Margery took Griff for a long walk. While they were out, Mrs. Owen phoned for news of the campers, and was invited over for tea in the afternoon.

Mrs. Furness had not mentioned Griff's presence over the telephone, and so Bron took him out with her to wait for the bus, in order to get the worst of the meeting over in private.

Mrs. Owen would not approach within a yard of Griff. She stood just inside the garden and speculated with horror what risks Bron had exposed herself to. Griff, knowing that she was afraid and made nervous by her emphatic gestures, began to growl softly.

'Bron, you must take that dog instantly and shut him up somewhere until the police can collect him. He is obviously completely savage and untrustworthy.'

Bron, slowly following her into the house, said with more confidence than she felt, 'But I really think that the army will let me keep him, Mother. Please say that I may. I promise that he wouldn't be a nuisance to you, and I love him such a lot already. I can't just let him go now.'

'You're a dreamer, Bronwen!' said Mrs. Owen, her voice rising with exasperation. 'Even you must realize how impossible it would be, to fit *that* dog into life in a small flat. It's quite out of the question!'

The three boys were out for tea, which was a good thing. Mrs. Owen would keep reverting to the subject of Griff and how he could not possibly be kept at the flat, but everyone except Anne realized why this was. Bron's mother knew that if Mrs. Furness had been in her place she would not have hesitated to accept Griff and would have managed perfectly well somehow. In that house, she felt guilty because she was not a dog-lover.

When the telephone rang, Dr. Furness came from his surgery to answer it, and then put his head round the door of the sitting-room where they were having tea.

'Forgot to tell you girls at lunch-time. I rang the police

this morning to let them know we've the dog here and they were pleased to let us keep him until the army decides what to do about the matter. They must have contacted the R.A.V.C. straight away, because they've just been on the phone. The dog's handler will be here on Tuesday to "see what the situation is", as they put it. All right? Let me know when you're ready to go, Mrs. Owen, and I'll take you into town. Got a call to make in that direction.'

Before she left, Bron's mother said to her quietly, 'I'm very sorry to disappoint you so much, but you must realize yourself that it wouldn't be fair to the dog either. Apart from his size, there's his uncertain temper as well as his deafness. He's a problem dog, isn't he? He wouldn't be happy, Bron, living in a small third-floor flat in the very middle of the town. You must tell his handler that you cannot consider keeping Griff, and that really is final.'

The next day was Sunday and a fine one. They left Bromfield at ten-thirty on the Shrewsbury bus, on their way to Joe's home for dinner and tea.

Bron had left Griff on a long tether by the side of the house, out of sight of the dalmatians, and hoped that he would not miss her too much. She didn't really want to go, but knew that Margery would be disappointed if she didn't. She felt very miserable, but tried hard not to show it and Joe's parents simply thought her rather quiet and shy.

In the afternoon they walked parallel to the Lawley, along Hoar Edge, and then down the valley to Caer Caradoc. Joe wanted to show them the Iron Age camp there, that he said was even bigger in extent than Nordy Bank and with more remaining of the fortification.

As they began to climb up the long sweep of the hill, they passed a small group of grazing ponies and were carefully

watched on their way by the herd stallion. Even Anne could find no fault with them. The stallion in particular was very beautiful, silver-grey and smooth coated, ears pricked in his rough mane, his heavy tail swinging below his hocks.

The bracken heads were just beginning to unroll, and the rough slope above them was tweeded with the yellow-red leaves of the little bilberry bushes and the pale green and yellow of the bogs. Etched against the sky were the

huge banks of the Iron Age camp and Margery looked
suddenly round at Bron, wondering if they ought to go on,
if the shadow would be there, too, as it had been at Nordy
Bank. She saw that Bron had no worry about that now
because she was thinking too much about Griff to have
room for it.

They went slowly up between the banks guarding the
gateway and came suddenly to the crest of the hill. The wind

staggered them backwards until they caught their balance and leant on to it.

The whole feeling of the hill was one of exhilaration. The flick and flurry of the wind spiced their skin until they felt their blood running warm. It was like standing on the back of a dragon, dwarfs on his backbone, feeling the rock ribs and spine hard beneath their feet. The hill-side fell away from them down to the valley, a precipitous sweep of grey and green, and the gold of a few scattered gorse-bushes far below.

With the wind in their heads like wine, they all turned together and charged down beside the banks to the bottom of the camp, where the narrow end of the hill faced towards the Wrekin and Shrewsbury somewhere beyond it. The lines of the fortifications were clear and impressive.

'I feel like an eaglet in its eyrie,' said Joe, squatting on the higher of the double banks.

'You ought to feel more like a dragonet in its nest,' said Margery. 'A red dragon of Wales. The Celts were being beaten back into Wales, weren't they? And fighting all the way.'

'Yes,' said Peter, looking sideways at Bron. 'It's easy to imagine the Celts manning this fortress: swarms of little wild people rushing about with woad on!'

'They were *not* little wild people and they did *not* rush about with woad on!' Bron stared at Peter indignantly, and then smiled when she realized that he was teasing her. 'No, but they didn't, Peter! They were brave, and just as civilized as we are now, in their own way. They made the most beautiful brooches and shields and things, all engraved and enamelled. In fact, in many ways they were more clever than we are now. All things considered.'

'All things considered!' repeated Joe, laughing. 'But

you're prejudiced, you know. Come over to the Stretton side, and I'll show you their water-hole.'

Bron and Margery climbed down to walk round between the banks, while the others went across the head of the hill. The Long Mynd lay along their horizon now, westward across the narrow valley. The high plateau was creased and crumpled and broken up by steep gullies along its near edge, but backed by the smooth moorland ridge down which ran one of the oldest green roads of England, the Portway. It seemed suddenly quite quiet and still, although the wind swooped overhead.

'These camps feel so forlorn to me,' said Margery, putting her hand against the side of the bank in passing. 'They have been *alone* for so long. The ruins of an old house are sad enough, but I just feel that these ruins are forlorn. They've a kind of strength and dignity, like some houses, but still— they are only a small remembrance of a people, aren't they? And some of the camps are forgotten.'

Bron smiled. 'But there are other remembrances, too— the lovely flint arrow-heads and tools of the earlier people, bronze ornaments and pottery things, sling stones and swords. All that, as well as the great camps and the old marked trails along the hills. Not really forlorn you know, nor forgotten, but just secret places now.'

Then they both laughed, because they seemed to have reversed the roles they had had on Nordy Bank. And then they remembered Griff.

At the beginning of the evening Mrs. Furness had suggested that Griff should be left outside to sleep in Lucy's empty kennel, instead of going upstairs with Bron. He had looked at her so savagely when she had taken his food to him in the middle of the day that she was afraid Mrs. Owen was right in thinking that it wasn't safe for Bron to be with him.

But Bron said firmly that if he *had* to go away soon, she wanted to be with him while she could, and in any case, he had been trained to accept only one person as his friend. At the moment, he accepted her. What would happen on Tuesday, when he saw his handler, she added regretfully, she didn't know. After that, perhaps, it would not be safe for her to be with him either.

They were all together in the sitting-room, except for Margery, who had disappeared about an hour after they had returned from Church Stretton. Dr. Furness was reading, Mrs. Furness knitting, Anne writing another letter, and the three boys playing Monopoly. Bron, well away from everyone, was gently brushing the mud out of Griff's thick coat on to an old sheet.

'Can I do a deal on hire-purchase?' inquired Robin hopefully. 'I want to buy Marylebone Station and I've only got three pounds.'

'I wonder where Margery is?' said Mrs. Furness, looking at the clock.

Margery was walking up the stairs to Bron's flat, behind Mr. Owen. She was rather nervous and she was out of breath.

After reassuring Mrs. Owen that Griff had been perfectly well-behaved all day and had shown no sign of attacking Bron, she sat on the edge of an arm-chair and wondered why she had come. Mrs. Owen thought she knew.

'If you've come to try to persuade me that there *is* room here for a large alsatian to be kept as a pet, then I'm really sorry, Margery, but it's no use. You must see that for yourself.'

Margery looked round the small square room crowded with too much heavy furniture, and nodded reluctantly.

'I've been worrying about it all day,' she said, 'because I can't bear the thought of Bron having to give Griff up. She's so terribly unhappy about it. He trusts her, you see, and she really does love him. I had an idea.' She paused.

Seeing that she had now rather lost confidence in this idea, Mr. Owen leaned forward and smiled at her encouragingly. 'Let's have it, then.'

'Well, it was just that perhaps you would let Bron keep Griff at Bromfield, until you move. Then you might have a larger flat next time. She could have Lucy's big outdoor kennel for him and I'm sure Mummy would let me make a little run in front of it. Then Bron could bike out after school to take him for a run, and I could do it for her quite often. I'm sure we could manage between us.'

She looked doubtfully at Mrs. Owen.

'It's kind of you to go to this trouble for her, Margery, but I can't agree to that either. The dog's trained to be savage and it's deaf into the bargain. I should never feel at ease about it. It would never be thoroughly trustworthy.'

'Could we leave that to the army to decide?' Mr. Owen looked thoughtful. 'It said in the newspaper that if the Canine Defence League School found themselves unable to give a report of absolute reliability, then the dog would be destroyed. They won't take any risks. You can be sure of that.'

'Well, even if the R.A.V.C. allow her to have the dog, and he *does* accept his re-training, I still can't think it a satisfactory solution, I'm afraid. For one thing, Bron can't be rushing out to Bromfield in all weathers to exercise the creature! Alsatians need such a lot of exercise, don't they? And for another, we'll be moving again in eight months,

Ian. What happens if we go to Manchester or Liverpool, or some other large city? Even if we found a flat large enough *and* a willing landlord, it wouldn't be fair to the dog. It's quite impossible!'

Margery sat very still in her chair, embarrassed and wondering if she ought to go. It was obvious that a family argument was rapidly developing.

Mr. Owen stood up. 'Well,' he said, smiling at her reassuringly, 'there's a lot to discuss. It was very kind of you to come, Margery. You're a good friend! Bron's lucky to have found you: she doesn't find many, moving about as we have to. Tell her that we'll come out to see her tomorrow evening. I'd like a word with your mother and father, too, if they can spare the time. And now, I'll take you home. It's getting late.'

15

If Anyone Can Do It . . .

They had had tea early, and so Margery thought that there would be time to take Griff for a shortish walk before Bron's parents arrived. Bron had been thoroughly miserable all day, certain that she was to be taken home that evening, leaving Griff at Bromfield. Then his handler would arrive in the morning, to be told that Griff must return with him. She would never see him again, nor know what had happened to him.

When they arrived back at the house, however, Mr. Owen's car was already parked on the verge and he was smoking his pipe beside the garden gate, waiting for them. Margery went quickly indoors while he was admiring Griff, thinking that he wanted to tell Bron in private that she quite definitely could not keep him.

Instead of that, he was telling Bron how kind Dr. and Mrs. Furness had been, and how lucky she was to have such a thoughtful friend as Margery. Griff could be boarded out at Bromfield, with a warm kennel and a wired run on the lawn at the side of the house.

'Mrs. Furness insists that he'll be no trouble to her, if you and Margery promise to do *all* the exercising. She says that with nine large dogs to feed already, one more won't make much difference.'

Bron stared at him incredulously. 'I can keep him! For always? But what about when we move?'

Mr. Owen frowned slightly. 'I can't say what will happen

then. You'll have to wait and see. I should have news of the
next posting in a few weeks' time, but it may be difficult.
In the meanwhile, you'll have eight months in which to
enjoy his company, so you must make the most of that.'

'Oh, I will!' Bron squatted to stroke Griff. 'It will be
wonderful! And eight months is nearly a year.'

'It's going to be hard work,' warned her father. 'You'll
have to give up most of your spare time in the school term,
you know. He needs a good walk *every* day. It will mean a lot
of bus journeys out to Bromfield and back, whatever the
weather.'

'Yes,' said Bron, feeling her first pleased sense of respon-
sibility, that the happiness and well-being of Griff would
depend upon *her* efforts. 'It will all be worth it.'

They had stayed up half the night, in celebration. Seeing
Bron so excited that she couldn't stop talking, both Peter
and Joe had remembered her as she had been on Nordy
Bank, sullen and aggressive, and wondered at the change in
her. Peter, watching her make ambitious plans for long
rambles with Margery, began to feel that perhaps Margery
had been right after all, in thinking that some spirit brooding over the hill had in a strange way affected her behaviour
there.

They all felt lazy in the morning, because of their late
night, but Bron and Margery took Griff for a long walk
before breakfast and then brushed him again afterwards in
the privacy of Margery's bedroom.

Bron had suddenly found, at the back of all her rejoicing,
the cold fact that Griff was not yet hers. The R.A.V.C.
might already have promised him to someone else, perhaps
to his handler, who must be fond of him, too. The school
that he had to attend might fail to break the habit of his

training. Then no one would have him, because he would be destroyed.

While she brushed him and tried to push the thought from her mind, Margery sat on the bed and talked hard in an effort to cheer her up.

'He looks beautiful now, Bron; not nearly so fierce and wolflike as he did on Nordy Bank. I shall always remember the wolves we saw at Whipsnade Zoo, the summer before last. They have a really big enclosure, with a wood in it, and we saw them as they were running between the trees. It made tingles on my spine; they looked so like a wild hunting pack.'

When she heard a car stop in the road outside and then the garden gate open, Margery scrambled along the bed to the window to see who it was. It was Corporal Smythe.

'I'll go and bring him up here, Bron. It'll be better than your bringing Griff down, because the others are all still messing about and then there's Lucy. Just you wait here.'

Bron put the brush away and sat nervously on the window-seat. Griff lay down.

When Margery had opened the bedroom door, she stood back to let Corporal Smythe go in, then closed it quietly behind him and went back downstairs.

Griff stood up hesitantly, but stayed beside Bron, his tail waving slowly to and fro. Corporal Smythe smiled at Bron, then said sharply, 'Heel!'

Griff went to him with his head held low, his tail half tucked between his legs, and his handler squatted to greet him, rubbing his ears gently and his neck hard. Griff butted him with his forehead and growled softly. Corporal Smythe looked up at Bron's anxious face and smiled again. 'Now call him back to you.'

'Griff,' she said firmly. 'Griff, come here!' He did go, but very slowly, looking round at his handler just before he reached her. Then he sat down, leaning slightly against her legs.

'Just about!' remarked the Corporal. 'I think he'd have stayed put, though, if I'd had him sitting properly at heel, but I won't try him at that with you. It would only confuse him. He'll be confused enough when he gets down to Gloucestershire.'

Without his cap, Corporal Smythe looked a young man, not a great deal older than Peter or Joe. He was very tall and the fair skin that went with his red hair was beginning to burn and freckle in the early summer sun. As Margery was saying, downstairs, 'with that hair and skin, he should have gone into the Navy. That horrid khaki doesn't suit

him at all.' Which remark disgusted Robin, Peter, and Joe.

Corporal Smythe sat beside Bron on the window-seat, so that Griff should have no worry as to whom he should stay by, and explained the situation to her.

The R.A.V.C. were offering Griff on payment of ten pounds and with the condition that he should attend the reform school run by the National Canine Defence League, for as long as was necessary. Their report on his character would decide his future and the army authority reserved the right to direct that he should be destroyed if the report could not guarantee him completely trustworthy.

'Oh, do you think he'll be all right?' Bron looked anxiously down at Griff. 'He's not at all friendly to any of the others, not even Margery.'

'Most alsatians are stand-offish with anyone outside their family circle,' he said reassuringly, 'and he's been especially taught to be suspicious of anybody but myself. I'm curious to know how you managed to get on such good terms with him in the first place.'

So Bron explained how near he'd been to starving and how she'd had him to herself for some time before the others returned.

'And anyway,' she said, 'dogs always do seem to like me, for some reason. I suppose they just know that I like *them*.'

He nodded. 'Yes, I see that, and also that I can give a good report on you, because, of course, he couldn't be offered to anyone unsuitable. If you do have him, though, you must make sure that he gets enough exercise—a long walk every day. Twice round the block and once to the corner's no use to him.'

When Corporal Smythe went downstairs for coffee, Robin spent some time in a valiant attempt to persuade him

to give a display of Griff's athletic talents in the garden, but
he refused.

'He's better left alone now. If I remind him of such par-
lour tricks as climbing a ten-foot wall, he might decide to
show you a few more when I've gone, and hold you flat
on your back in a state of terror for a couple of days!'

He left without seeing Griff again.

To Bron, the third part of the journey to Bristol seemed
never-ending. The bus was lurching slowly along at what
felt like five miles an hour, and Griff was half asleep on the
floor between her feet. He was muzzled, but had behaved
himself really quite well, she thought, all things considered.
A few people had made rude remarks about him, thinking
it not safe to have him on a public vehicle, and she had had
to prevent several more from patting him. He had been
very nervous on the way to Hereford, but had gradually
become used to the uneven motion of the top deck of a
double-decker bus.

Bron's mother had wanted to drive them down in the
car, but Mr. Owen had needed it to keep an appointment in
Bishop's Castle. Then she had wanted to go down with them
herself. Corporal Smythe had advised Bron to take Griff
by bus, as there was less noise and confusion than by rail.
This meant three changes and Mrs. Owen had been sure
that Bron would go off in the wrong direction. Finally
Bron had been able to persuade her that she would not, and
in any case would much prefer to be on her own.

She had enjoyed the ride from Hereford to Gloucester:
through Ross-on-Wye, where the river was much wider
than she had expected it to be, and along the edge of the
sheltered Forest of Dean, where the trees were already
in full leaf. But the road from Gloucester to Bristol

was surprisingly dull, perhaps because she was beginning to grow nervous and rather tired of the slow pace of the bus.

In Bristol, she became suddenly panic-stricken when surrounded by the tumble and bustle of the busy city. Although she knew perfectly well which bus she should catch to take her out to the school, she walked straight up to the queue of waiting taxis. When she was sitting comfortably in the comparative quiet of one, she became part of the bustle herself instead of merely an outsider confused by it, and felt immediately more secure and happy.

By the time they reached the cluster of small bungalows, sheds, and wired runs that was the school, both Bron and Griff were less nervous.

A friendly girl who Bron thought must be a kennel-maid walked with her from the gate, settled her into a small and comfortable but empty office, and told her to wait there. Griff sat, suspiciously alert, with his ears pricked, and snarled when the door suddenly opened and a man came in, whistling loudly.

'Well, my boy, that's nice reception to give the head-master!' he said, shaking his head at Griff and smiling at Bron. 'I'd have come in a little less noisily if I'd known I had nervous visitors. Or rather *a* nervous visitor. You're not nervous, are you? Is it Miss Owen?'

'No,' said Bron. 'I mean, no, I'm not nervous. Yes, I am Miss Owen. I mean, I'm Bron.'

'Bron.' He walked across to shake hands with her. 'How do you do? I'm Neil Kirby. Trainer-in-charge, I suppose you could call me.'

Griff stopped snarling and sat stiffly. Mr. Kirby stood still and looked down at him.

'A fine dog. It amazes me that he has accepted you so

quickly. Will you take off the muzzle, please, Bron? I'm looking forward to working with him, especially as he has the additional problem of deafness. We've never had an army dog in here before.'

'What sort of dogs do you have in?' Bron knelt down beside Griff.

'Oh, all shapes, sizes and conditions. I'll show you round in a while, after we've had our cup of tea. We have had two completely deaf dogs in the past, but, of course, he has the army upbringing to forget about as well.'

The nice kennel-maid came into the office then, bringing two cups of tea, and a dish of water for Griff.

'He's had quite a long journey, hasn't he?' she said. 'I thought he'd be glad of it.'

While they drank their tea, Bron told Mr. Kirby about the camp on Nordy Bank and Griff's three appearances there before he finally came to her. She didn't mention that she had driven him away each time before that, because of course she couldn't explain why she had done it. He was very interested, especially so as he knew the area well himself, having been born in Bridgnorth.

After that, they settled Griff into a kennel with a long wired run in front of it.

'There are a few doubtful characters about the place,' explained Mr. Kirby. 'Dogs, I mean, though, not people. I don't want him to start by disgracing himself and fighting some ferocious inmate to the death.'

As they walked round, he told her the case histories of some of the dogs. Some had been confirmed child-biters, having been tormented by children at some time, or made jealous by the birth of children into a childless family. One very savage-looking alsatian had been trained by its owner to attack anything that moved.

'Leo is taking some time to reform, I'm afraid,' remarked Mr. Kirby, stopping in front of the pen. 'The training he had was pretty brutal and the poor dog was soured by it. We've had him here for six months already and I'm not sure that we can save him now.'

Bron asked anxiously, 'Will you need to keep Griff as long as that? He'll have forgotten me by then! Do you think he'll be all right, Mr. Kirby?'

He shook his head. 'Well, I can't really say much at this stage. It may take a month or it may take a year. I should be hopeful, but not over-confident, if I were you, Bron. He's certainly not as embittered as Leo, for example. You can see that by looking at him. He's got a good basic character, or he wouldn't have trusted you so soon. Don't worry about his forgetting you, though. I can promise you he won't do that.'

There were, as he had said, all shapes and sizes of dogs. Bron saw various small terriers, sheep-dogs, alsatians, spaniels, and labradors. One golden labrador ran eagerly down her pen as they passed by and Mr. Kirby took Bron in with him to fuss her properly.

'She seems a very nice dog,' said Bron in surprise.

'Oh yes, she is, but she was going to be destroyed until we heard about the case and fought it for her. So she was sent to reform school instead!'

'What did she do?'

'Only bit two people rather badly. But we thought she had good reason for doing so, because it was in defence of her puppies. Labradors are seldom vicious, you know. They're very good-natured.'

Bron was also introduced to eight huskies, veterans from Antarctic expeditions, who crowded round her, pushing and shoving each other to get closer to Mr. Kirby.

'And these are supposedly untameable!' he said, laughing at their enthusiasm. 'We're very fond of them. The experts were sure that the wild pack instinct developed in a team to such an extent that you could never trust them afterwards.'

Bron was surprised, on returning to the office, to find that she had been watching the work of the school for more than two hours. When Mr. Kirby realized that she was going home on the 5.35 train from Bristol and had only had sandwiches on the bus for her lunch, he insisted on taking her to his own home for tea.

Bron enjoyed herself very much there and didn't feel in the least shy, which was most unusual for her. Mrs. Kirby wanted to hear about Griff and Nordy Bank, too, and they all talked so busily that it was five o'clock before tea was finished. Mr. Kirby said that he had to go down into Bristol sometime, so he may as well go now and take Bron straight to Temple Meads station.

Bron was very much relieved to hear this, having begun to panic at the thought of missing her train. 'Oh, thank you!' she said. 'Have I time to say good-bye to Griff, please?' And although she didn't say it aloud, she thought it: 'In case I never see him again.'

Mr. Kirby hesitated. 'You do have time, just about, but I don't advise it. He'll have resigned himself to being alone again by now and it would only unsettle him. But if you want to very badly, then, of course, you can.'

Bron thought quickly and said that no, she didn't want to unsettle him, and so they set off down the long hill to the city.

The streets were seething. Late shoppers forged through the outward flow of pedestrians homeward bound, and the road throbbed with a frustrated medley of vehicles: cars, delivery vans, bicycles and lorries, buses crammed with passengers—the illegal overloaders on the platform all either trying to avoid the enraged eye of the busy conductor or to persuade him that, as they were only going to the next stop anyway, it wasn't worth his bothering to turn them off.

Bron was tremendously thankful that Mr. Kirby had brought her down, especially when she saw by the station clock that it was almost half past five. They reached the platform just as the train was announced and he smiled at her and said good-bye.

'I can't absolutely promise anything, you understand, but don't turn your hair grey with worry, will you? It's a tricky thing to safely undo two years of thorough training, but we've had plenty of experience and if anyone can do it, we can!'

16

Ready and Waiting

When the noise and rush of the station was over, the usual constrained silence fell on the crowded compartment. Those without the comfort of a newspaper stared into space; Bron stared out of the window.

She had been so impressed by the work of the school that while she was with Mr. Kirby she had felt quite happy and confident. Now the confidence began to leave her. The weather was no help. Mist hung low along the estuary and tumbled among the trees. The big hills round Abergavenny were quite invisible. When she glanced at the other passengers, they all appeared to be either fast asleep or full of their own worries. Bron was glad to change trains at Hereford.

The little local diesel was warm and noisy and altogether more cheerful. By the time it buzzed into Ludlow station, Bron had convinced herself that Griff would emerge from his un-training with flying colours. After all, she seemed fated to own him! He had found his way to Nordy Bank and come to her when she was alone. For his sake, she had made the effort to overcome the power of the strange shadow that had moved in her there. Now she had been given the chance to keep him for eight months, at least—and she felt sure at that moment that she would do so.

It was raining heavily as she left the station and she ran quickly across to the wicket gate which led to the short cut up through the town. A car moved slowly in front of her and her father leaned from the window.

'Taxi, lady?'

She got in thankfully. 'Ugh! What a night! I hope they put plenty of straw in Griff's kennel. It's freezing!'

'I always feel freezing, too, when I leave one of those cosy little diesels,' he agreed. 'I'm as warm as toast myself. Thought your train got in at nine, until your mother came back and told me it was twenty to. Had to run like a mad rabbit across the town to the garage. The *next* time we move, I shall make quite certain that there is a vacant garage at a reasonable distance from the flat. I wasn't built to be a long-distance runner!'

'Oh, I've just had a wonderful idea!' said Bron, excitedly. 'We could keep Griff in there, too, as well as the car! There'd be plenty of room for a kennel. Then it won't matter how big the flat is, will it?'

'I don't somehow think that an alsatian would enjoy living in a garage in the middle of Liverpool, or somewhere similar,' he said, after a short silence, 'but as I said before— you must just wait and see what comes. Don't fly your hopes too high.'

A month passed much more quickly than Bron had expected. She spent a lot of time at Bromfield, helping to exercise the dogs and watching the puppies grow. Anne had returned home to Bristol, but received regular bulletins on the progress of the smallest puppy, Spotted Dick. When Peter suggested that he should move Lucy's old kennel round to the side of the house in readiness for Griff, both Margery and Bron thought that this would be an unlucky thing to do, inviting Fate to decide that they shouldn't have him after all. So no preparations were made.

At the end of the month Bron received a short letter from Mr. Kirby, to say that Griff was making as much progress

N.B.—K

as could be expected, but that he would have to stay at the school for a further two or three months, before a report could be issued.

She read this letter so many times that it finally took on a slightly sinister and depressing tone. 'As much progress as could be expected', was a very cautious way to put it—the kind of statement made by hospitals when they didn't want to raise your hopes too high. In any case, Griff would have forgotten her by the time the course was over; it would perhaps be four months since he had last seen her, before he saw her again. Even if he did come, the summer would be almost over and they would be leaving Ludlow in January.

Everybody tried hard to cheer Bron up. Perhaps because she had been unreasonably confident before, she now had little faith in Griff's return and moped all over the place. Then her depression seemed to spread to her mother, and Bron was aware of a continuous atmosphere of anxiety between her parents. When she was in bed, she often heard through the thin wall of the partition the steady drone of suppressed argument, and thought that her mother was still against her owning Griff for even a short time. Then, after an unexpected visit from Dr. and Mrs. Furness while Bron was out with Margery, the feeling of worry suddenly left the flat and several excursions were arranged to distract her thoughts from the waiting.

They went shopping in Birmingham. They went for a day to the Wild Fowl Trust at Slimbridge, which was not far from Gloucester. They went to the Elan Valley reservoirs. They went away for the week-end to Snowdonia and took Margery with them.

When they returned, a long, stiff, official-looking envelope was lying on the hall table, addressed to Miss Bronwen Owen.

Bron picked it up casually and put it unopened into her pocket.

'I think I'll go and ring up Margery,' she said, 'to see if anyone has come home yet. She'll be lonely.'

They had taken Margery straight to Bromfield on their return, but found the house empty. As she had a key with her, they had gone in and found a note explaining that the whole family had taken the dogs out for a walk, but would not be away for long. So Margery had stayed.

Mrs. Owen peeped round the front door to see which way Bron went. She turned left, walking quickly through the neat gardens before the curtain wall of the castle, and began to run just before she turned in between the walls down towards the little postern gate.

'Well?' said Mr. Owen. 'Telephone?'

Mrs. Owen shut the door and went back into the hall. 'No. Quite the wrong direction! She'll have rushed away to her favourite seat, the one almost hidden in the grass that looks towards Whitcliffe. Oh, I do hope it's good news!'

Bron's eyes returned to the two words which seemed to stand out from all the others on the page—*perfectly satisfactory*. She heaved a huge sigh of relief, stretched her arms above her head and said aloud, 'Oh, Griff, how lovely! How glorious!' Meeting the astonished eyes of two visitors gazing up at the castle towers from the path below, she laughed, called, 'Good afternoon! Isn't it a gorgeous day?' turned and ran back at full speed out into Dinham.

Her mother had hardly taken off her coat and put the kettle on, before Bron swirled into the flat, shouting, 'It's all right! Griff's passed! When can I go down to fetch him? Can I go tomorrow?'

After the confusion of joy and congratulations had died down a little, Mrs. Owen made the tea.

'I really don't think that you can go tomorrow,' she said. 'You'll have to have permission from school, won't you? If you telephone Mr. Kirby early in the morning, perhaps he would put Griff on the train for you, and you could meet him at the station in the evening.'

'No.' Mr. Owen was reading the letter, which was from the Headquarters of the R.A.V.C. 'They want Bron to go down to Bristol herself, so that the trainer can explain the commands Griff is used to obeying now, and so on.'

'And anyway,' said Bron, 'I couldn't just let him arrive *alone*. I want to fetch him home myself. Can I go on Tuesday, then? We're down on the field all afternoon so I shan't miss much. It doesn't matter about games.'

'I think it would be better not to rush things,' said Mrs. Owen. 'Leave it until Saturday. You've the kennel and the run to fix up at Bromfield, haven't you? And dog brushes and a collar and leash to buy. You'll have to visit the Post Office to draw out some of your savings.'

Bron began to protest that a whole week was too long to wait, but her father said firmly, 'You've waited two months already; another week can't make much difference. Write and let Mr. Kirby know that you'll arrive on Saturday morning.'

Bron fidgeted about all week and again her mother seemed to catch the feeling. She went out to Bromfield several times with Bron, had long talks with Mrs. Furness and helped her with her gardening. The wired run and the kennel were soon in position, sheltered between the side of the house and the garden hedge. By Thursday, there was nothing left to do but wait.

On Saturday, Bron left the flat at half past seven to catch the seven forty-eight train, which would get into Bristol at eleven fifteen. As the train drew away from the town the smooth shape of the Titterstone Clee surged against the pale blue-yellow of the early-morning sky. The wooded slopes of the High Vinnalls, the Goggin, and Croft Ambrey were to the west.

Bron remembered Nordy Bank as she stared first at the Clee and then at Croft Ambrey. There had been Iron Age forts on both these hills, and the excavations at Croft Ambrey had disclosed bronze fittings and ornaments, spindle whorls and swords. Nordy Bank had never been excavated and, thinking about it now, she was glad. It seemed better to leave its life buried and secret and some-how, more dignified.

The city was as busy and alive as ever, it being the middle of Saturday morning, but Bron found her way out to the school with no difficulty. There didn't seem to be anybody about and she was tempted to go quietly on her own round to the kennel where she had last seen Griff. It would be safer to greet him first while she was alone with him, to avoid showing her disappointment too clearly if he did not remember her.

It was fortunate that she decided that this would not perhaps be very polite. As she walked up the path to Mr. Kirby's office, the door opened and he looked out.

'Hello!' he said cheerfully. 'I heard the gate close and thought it would be you. He's ready and waiting. Come inside.'

He held the door open for her, and as she went through, she saw Griff.

He came to her before she called him and pushed hard round and round her legs, tossing his tail in a circle rather than wagging it, and whining loudly in a squeaky and excited way.

'Did you think he had forgotten you?' asked Mr. Kirby kindly, seeing the relief in Bron's face. 'Alsatians are one-man dogs at heart, you know, although he'll tolerate other people from now on because we've taught him good manners. He'll grow to be quite friendly with a few, I expect, but mostly he'll just be polite.'

The trainer demonstrated the words of command that he had been using with Griff, and the gestures that took the place of these if the dog should be too far away to hear.

'Draw his attention first by whistling,' he explained. 'Our vet doesn't think that the deafness will develop much more now, and he's certain that he'll never be wholly deaf. So he shouldn't be much of a problem to you from that point of view. The difficulty is more likely to be in exercising him sufficiently to keep him out of mischief.'

Time slipped by very quickly. Mr. Kirby insisted on taking Bron home with him for dinner, explaining that his wife wanted to say good-bye to Griff. He then drove her

down to the station in time to catch the two twenty-five to
Hereford.

The bustle and clatter of Temple Meads seemed not to
upset Griff at all. He followed closely at Bron's heels with
great self-possession and Mr. Kirby seemed very pleased
with him.

They had not long to wait for the train, which was only
ten minutes late, and they said good-bye as it came slowly up
to the platform. Bron promised Mr. Kirby, after she had
thanked him, that she would bring Griff to see him when
the family next came through Bristol, which they did quite
frequently on the way to visit her grandparents.

Bron walked slowly along the platform, looking for a
fairly empty compartment with pleasant-looking people in
it. She found one near the front of the train, and went in.

'Excuse me,' she said shyly, 'but would you mind if I
brought my dog in with me? He'll be quite quiet.'

'Not at all,' replied the middle-aged woman, who had the
firmly benevolent look of a schoolmistress.

The young man glanced up over the top of his newspaper, saw Griff and put it down on his knees.

'Well, he is a beauty! Much better keep him in here than
stick him in the guard's van. How old is he?'

Bron needed no encouragement to talk about Griff and
the telling of his story kept all three of them entertained for
a good part of the journey.

17

Looking Towards the Clee

The church clock struck the quarter as Bron walked up past the sweet smell of the granary towards the town. A quarter past five. The Shrewsbury diesel had been in a few minutes early, so perhaps that was why Margery had not been at the station to meet them. She would probably meet them on the way.

Bron looked repeatedly to make herself believe that Griff was there, safe and happy and her own. Since no one was coming down the footpath to the station, she stopped two or three times to talk to him, rubbing behind his ears when he pushed his head hard against her legs.

Waiting to cross the main road at the Bull Ring, she noticed several people watching him admiringly, because it was obvious that he was beautifully trained. Safe in the plump arms of his mistress, an excited white poodle chittered abuse, but Griff ignored it. Bron was so proud to be with him that she had to keep pushing an idiotically broad smile from her face, trying to look as though she were quite accustomed to walking through the town with a very large and very handsome grey alsatian following closely at her heels.

Margery did not appear. Bron was disappointed, but ran quickly up the stairs to the flat, thinking that she might be having tea there with her parents. After all, she hadn't said definitely whether it was this train or the later one that she would come on.

Her mother and father were alone in the sitting-room. The table was laid for tea.

'Here he is!' announced Bron, anxiously, feeling suddenly rather shy and very much afraid that her parents would take no pleasure at all in seeing Griff again. He was so beautiful, and so obedient that she could not understand how anyone could fail to admire him now.

He *was* admired: whole-heartedly by her father, and a little nervously at first by her mother. When he lay down quietly on the hearth-rug, however, and showed no inclination to move without being told to, Mrs. Owen breathed a large sigh of relief and went into the kitchen to make the tea.

Bron, as relieved as she was, instantly forgot all her anxiety and began to talk excitedly about what Mr. Kirby had told her of Griff's training. Her father listened politely with his face, but his eyes watched her with a different expression, as if he were intent only upon his own thoughts. Her anxiety returned.

During tea, Mr. Owen explained the situation—the reason for the many hidden arguments that Bron had sensed before she heard from the R.A.V.C. that Griff was finally her own. The new posting was to Paris!

There were four alternatives, he said. After talking things over between themselves, they had decided that the final choice must be Bron's. She was old enough now to know what she wanted and must tell them honestly what she thought was the best thing to do.

Firstly, they could take a flat in Paris and send Bron to an English school there. That would mean, no Griff. They would be lucky even to find a flat large enough for three people: accommodation was very hard to come by and very expensive. Also, the quarantine regulations would make holidays impossible, if he came too.

Secondly, Bron could attend a boarding school in England and travel over to Paris for the holidays. There was one school in particular which allowed what it called 'reasonable pets'. They might possibly have a vacant place in September.

Thirdly, Mrs. Owen could look for a larger flat in Ludlow, and Bron could stay on at the High School *and* have Griff at home. Then Mr. Owen would live in Paris for two years, on his own.

Fourthly, Bron could stay on at Ludlow, but alone. Dr. and Mrs. Furness had extended their kind hospitality to her, as well as to Griff. So she could live with Margery at Bromfield during term-time and leave Griff there for the school holidays, when she would go to Paris.

That was all. The decision must be Bron's. They had their own preference, naturally, but they were not going to discuss the alternatives with her because it was better that she should think things out for herself.

Mr. Owen fell forward across the table in mock exhaustion after such a serious speech. Her mother smiled anxiously at Bron.

'Don't worry about it for too long, dearest,' she said. 'Just decide what would make you most happy. It's a great pity that you can't have both, your friends here and Griff, *and* our normal family life, but it can't be helped.'

Bron finished her tea in a shocked silence. Everything had seemed beautifully simple half an hour ago: true, it would only have been so until January, but she was used to living in the present. Now she had to think very hard about the future. She put on her coat again in a daze, because Griff must be taken to Bromfield and settled for the night.

She had to wait for ten minutes at the Shrewsbury bus-stop, because the bus was late. She stood perfectly still, her father's words tumbling about in her mind. When the bus came over the top of the hill at the Bull Ring, she looked down at Griff, standing quietly beside her on the pavement, not nearly as wolflike now as he had been when he stood poised beyond the firelight on the bank above her, almost two months ago. She remembered how he had come to her on Nordy Bank. Her whole life had changed since that day. She wanted to keep him more than she had ever wanted anything before.

Sitting on the bus, she discarded one alternative without hesitation. Her father couldn't live alone in Paris: it would be horribly selfish to expect that. And she realized how afraid she was of the idea of going to a boarding school, because she had never made friends easily. Her choice was halved.

When she walked up the path to the front door, it opened before she reached it and the entire Furness family came out to meet Griff. He was admired and spoken to by everyone, rather cautiously at first, until they saw what a marked change there was in his behaviour. They were very impressed. Margery was quite beside herself with excitement.

'He is so handsome!' she exclaimed, kneeling to stroke him. 'It's the way he holds his head now. He kept his head and his tail down before, as though all the time he was half afraid.'

'I'm sure that he was.' Mrs. Furness smiled very kindly at Bron. 'Everything was confusing for him then, and Bron was the only person he trusted. Now he has the world in perspective and he knows what's expected of him.'

Bron wished that she knew what was expected of her. She saw that Dr. Furness was watching her, and wondered if she should say something about the possibility of coming to live with them. Then the moment passed. He patted her on the back and went indoors.

Robin followed him and ran out again with an envelope in his hand. 'It's a greetings telegram for Griff!' he explained, passing it over to Bron. 'From Anne.'

'She's coming up next week-end to collect her pudding-dog,' said Peter, 'and Joe's calling in tomorrow morning to see the wolf, so shades of Nordy Bank should creep upon you. Will they, do you think?'

'No,' replied Bron firmly, and smiled at Margery.

A grey and orange sunset blazed across the western sky, throwing wild bronze reflections along the river valleys and across the Clee. Bron left the bus at the bottom of Corve Street and walked back up Linney, to give herself more time to think.

She didn't usually mind such a lot moving from one town to another, because she was quite used to it. Her father had always worked for the same firm and so it had always happened. But Ludlow was different.

As she walked up the sloping gravel path towards the castle walls, she realized how much she would miss it all, not just the town itself and the friends she had made there, but the high hills and the kind feeling of belonging that they gave to her. It would be wonderful to live at Bromfield, with Griff, and to share Margery's family.

And then, standing below the castle, looking out across the Clun Forest and the Stretton hills, she knew that she couldn't stay. She must give it all up, and Griff too. She must take him back to Bristol next week, before he grew any more fond of her, and ask Mr. Kirby to find someone who would love and be kind to him. How could she say to her own parents—'I'd rather stay with someone else's family than go with you to Paris'?

Her mother was putting her coat on as Bron went into the sitting-room, and said cheerfully, 'We thought you'd be on that bus. Shall we all walk over Whitcliffe to watch the sun set?'

Bron nodded, and then as her father came in from the kitchen, said loudly, 'I'll take Griff away again. I'm coming with you.' Something hard and tight in her throat prevented her saying another word.

Her mother kissed her quietly and looked as though she felt like crying too. Her father said, 'Good girl! But you know, we didn't tell you *our* preference, did we, and that wasn't really fair.

'We'd like you to stay here. Of course we'll miss you very much indeed; you know that. But there'll be plenty of long holidays to look forward to, and you'll be very happy at Bromfield, with Griff and Margery. It'll do you good, too, mixing with people and being more independent. You'd like to stay, Bron, wouldn't you?'

She nodded, beginning to smile, but looking anxiously at her mother.

Mrs. Owen turned away to rummage in her hand-bag for the door-key. 'Yes, it is best,' she said, after a moment. 'We're all very fond of Ludlow and you really do need to settle down in one school now. You can't keep on changing every two years, as you have been doing. It isn't a very satisfactory life.'

'And Margery would be so dreadfully disappointed if you didn't stay. She's managed to persuade her mother that her bedroom will need redecorating, if you're to share it, and she's even chosen the wallpaper!' Bron's father pulled her hair in passing and opened the door. 'And now, put your best foot forward! It'll be dawn before we get out, at this rate.'

They went down through the old town gate to Ludford bridge, and then stood in one of the coigns on it, because the traffic lights changed when they were half-way over and there were several large lorries waiting to cross. Since the bridge was medieval, it did very well to take even single-line traffic. The river was low for lack of rain and shadowed from all last traces of the sun by Whitcliffe. The broken water round the islands shone in the dusk and the earnest fishermen along Bread Walk began to think regretfully of going home.

As they walked slowly up the steep path to the top of the common, Bron thought ahead into January. She was suddenly cold and panic-stricken by the idea of saying good-bye to her parents for so long. Peter was almost grown-up; he had been very sarcastic to her on Nordy Bank and surely wouldn't forget her behaviour there. She was also slightly afraid of Dr. Furness, who was so unlike her own father. She hurried to catch up with her mother, who would immediately understand her fears and comfortably insist on her accompanying them to France. But her parents were standing together to watch the sun go down.

The brilliance of gold and grey had softened and faded. The Brown Clee was dark against the sky, the blue of which was half hidden by ripples of thin pink cloud, ribbed like sand at a low tide. The sun shone bright on the quarry faces behind the head of Titterstone and on the beauty of the church tower, which rose far up into sunlight when the houses of the town below were dark. The grey walls of the castle, standing high above the river, began to lose their gilding.

Bron started to say, 'I think that I shall be too lonely

without you', but her parents had turned away to walk on. The words were lost in the rustle of bracken and the murmur of the three weirs breaking the flow of the Teme below them. She stood still, to be alone, feeling the beginning of pride in herself as a person old enough to make decisions. She realized suddenly that it would be easier to go to Paris than to stay behind, but that her parents would be disappointed in her if she did so.

She stared after them and found mist growing slowly from amongst the trees of the forest called *Mortimer*. Bron had always thought that a splendid name, conjuring up as it did the story of battles and bitter feuds between the Marcher Lords. From there many miles of woodland stretched away westward, over Bringewood Chase, Mary

Knoll, the High Vinnalls and the Goggin, to Wigmore
Rolls and the darkly wooded hills along the River Lugg. A
long silence of trees. A slow prickle began in her blood, as
it had on that first day in the camp on Nordy Bank.

She turned quickly to move on, but looked backwards
towards the Clee without wanting to. Along the flanks of
Titterstone the village lights were strung like necklaces,
but the hill reared its wave-crest head up dark into the
darkness. The brooding shape of the Brown Clee seemed to
be withdrawn into itself, humped and secretive. Nordy
Bank was there, but it belonged to the hill's past now and
she belonged to herself.

Bron thought of all the things she had to say to Margery
and wondered if there would still be time to telephone. She
began to run fast down the road after her parents, impatient
to be home again. There was so much to look forward to.